HIS QUIET AGENT

ADA MARIA SOTO

ROOKERY

Rookery Publishing
www.rookerypublishing.com

Written in New Zealand

First Printing: October 2017
Second Printing: February 2019
Ada Maria Soto

Paperback ISBN-13 978-0-473-41620-1

CONTENTS

For all the weird kids who sat alone at lunch.

ACKNOWLEDGMENTS

With eternal thanks to Nick for the never-ending support. My parents, who got to read this one. Cooper for the ass kicking, and Lynn and Kim and Jeff for the edits. And an extra thanks to the RWNZ Auckland chapter for the help, advice, and being really cool about the general boys kissing stuff. Even though the boys don't actually kiss in this one.

CHAPTER ONE

THERE WAS something about ficus trees Arthur found discon-
certing. It was how he could never tell if they were real or plastic.
It would irritate him to the point where he would break a leaf
trying to work it out, usually just at the moment when someone
important walked into the room. He restrained himself this time.
He would have thought that The Agency would have better quality
office plants, but since everyone who walked through the door had
to go through ten levels of security checks for each floor, it was
probably easier to go with plastic ficus. Maybe there were better
quality plants on higher floors. Hopefully, he would find out.

The office door opened and his supervisor looked out. "Agent
Drams?"

Arthur leapt to his feet. "Yes, sir."

"Come on in."

He followed the other, slightly more senior, agent into the tidy
office. It had a thin window that looked over the parking garage,
but that was more of a view than Arthur got from his cubicle.

"Sit down."

When Arthur first got his job with the Agency, he'd spent
hours practicing undoing the single button of his jacket one
handed while sitting smoothly. It was something he'd used only
three times, as the dress code among the analysts was a good deal
more relaxed than he had expected.

Agent Brown flipped open a file. "I received your promotion request."

"Yes, sir." It had been four years and Arthur felt he was due.

"It has been decided that your request will be granted. Tomorrow you will be moving up to the fifth floor as a level two analyst."

Arthur's excited 'thank you' died in his throat. "I'm already a level two analyst?"

His supervisor looked in his file again. "So, you are. But you'll be a level two analyst on the fifth floor."

"That's..." Arthur didn't want to rock the boat, complain or seem ungrateful, but it *had* been four years. "A bit more of a lateral move than I was expecting."

His supervisor sighed. "Agent Drams, no one knows who you are."

"We're a black budget government agency. No one is supposed to know who we are."

"To the general public yes, however, when your supervising agent and the promotion board have to ask 'who' at seeing your name and don't even recognize your picture, you need to show your admittedly somewhat generic face a bit more. This is your entire file." Agent Brown lifted three pieces of paper. "No notes against, no notes for, no citations, accolades or recommendations, no warnings, no nothing."

Arthur didn't know what to say. He'd kept his head down, worked hard.

"Tomorrow, report to Agent Collins on the fifth floor and... I don't know, volunteer to run the Super Bowl pool."

"I don't know anything about football."

"You don't need to."

"Okay. Thank you, sir." It was all Arthur could think to say. He didn't bother trying to button his coat as he left the office.

———

ARTHUR SUPPOSED if there was an upside to working for a secret government agency it was that he didn't have to call his parents and have them ask if he'd gotten a promotion. They thought he worked in industrial shipping insurance.

"Hey, Jude." He tapped the head of the small saint statue that sat next to his permanently unfinished five-a-side Rubik's Cube. Both graduation gifts from Hanh and his sisters. Personalization of work spaces wasn't encouraged, but most people had at least one thing on their desk. Stress balls and red staplers were popular.

He checked the time on his computer. Not even ten in the morning yet. Way too early to be able to justify leaving or even heading to lunch. Instead, he typed in his twenty-character password, brought up a selection of strangely worded, half-mad reports from field agents, and began to read.

————

THE HUMAN resources department, in conjunction with security, did whatever it was they did and Arthur's key card sent the elevator directly to the 5th floor. He stepped out and looked around. There were two ficus trees flanking the elevator doors. Taking a guess that the fifth floor was laid out the same as the fourth, he quickly found the office of Agent Collins. He knocked on the door. The call to enter was instantaneous.

"Hello, I'm Agent Drams, I've been assigned to you." He'd put on his best suit for the second day running.

"Sit-down."

Arthur sat, carefully undoing the button.

"I received your file yesterday. It's..." The senior agent trailed off.

"Brief?"

"That works." He looked over Arthur. Arthur returned the scrutiny. He wondered if agents at a certain level were clones. White, late 40's, slightly graying hair, small hunch in the posture from too many years sitting in front of a computer. "You were a level two analyst and now you're *my* level two analyst. There's an empty cubicle at the end of the row to your left as you head out. Your assignments will be in your inbox when you log in."

"Thank you, sir." A silence hung in the air as Arthur waited to be dismissed. "Do you have anyone running a Super Bowl pool up here?" Arthur hated football but he couldn't handle another sideways promotion, even if that meant sticking his head up.

"Agent Sims used to do it, but he bashed a fax machine to death with a three-hole punch, then quit. So, that's an open position, as it were."

"That's good to know."

Agent Collins turned to his computer and Arthur took it as his cue to leave.

There was the hum of the air conditioning, little computer fans, and the click of keyboards providing a background soundtrack as he walked down the row of cubicles. Classified government agencies were thankfully immune to the open plan office trend.

He found the empty cubicle and sat in the generic gray swivel chair. He never expected to be James Bond when he took the job, but he'd never expected it to feel so '90s corporate. He pulled his Rubik's cube and St. Jude out of his box. "Home sweet home." He started to log in.

"Why are you in my cubicle?"

Arthur swiveled around. At the entrance to the cubicle was a pale, slim man in a dark gray, almost-black suit with a dark gray, almost-black tie holding a dark gray, almost-black coffee cup.

"Um... I was told to take the empty cubicle?"

"This cubicle is not empty." The man's voice was emotionless, like a computer stating a fact.

Arthur looked around. Aside from the standard computer terminal the space was completely barren.

"The empty cubicle is there." The man pointed to a cubicle across the narrow hallway.

"Oh, sorry. I thought..." He trailed off. The man's face was still but his eyes made it very clear he did not want to talk and didn't like people in his space. Arthur grabbed Jude and his Rubik's cube and scurried across the hall.

So much for making friends.

CHAPTER TWO

ON THE second day, Arthur tried to ignore the man in the cubicle across the hall. Instead, at 12:30 he rolled his shoulders back, put on a smile which he'd been told was nice, and made his way to the lunch room. There was a large cafeteria in the basement, but agents who didn't want to risk government chicken salad congregated in the lunch room of their particular floor.

His plan was to wait until most of the tables had at least one person sitting at each, which would force him to introduce himself to someone and ask to share a table. He knew it would be painful, but he wanted to work on a floor that had real plants instead of plastic ones. Of course, the really hard bit was that in this job you didn't talk about anything personal. You didn't ask someone if they were married or had kids. Opening conversation topics were limited to local sports teams and recent, but not too recent, movie releases. And Arthur still hadn't managed to see the newest Marvel offering.

Most of the tables were half to completely full. He spotted a six seat one that had three seats free. He could sit in the middle of the three without elbowing anyone. He walked up, attempting to show confidence but not arrogance. "Anyone sitting here?"

The three guys looked up at him. One gestured to the middle seat. "Thanks." He sat quickly, having left his jacket in his cube. "Arthur," he offered.

"Jack," the guy in the middle replied but didn't offer his hand.

Arthur nodded. The guys hadn't been talking when he arrived so he couldn't add to a conversation. He went to open his mouth to say something but the words caught in his throat. None of them looked at him, focused instead on their own lunches. He gave an internal sigh while mentally kicking himself and did the same. One looked at him for an extra second when he pulled chopsticks and Gỏi cuốn rolls out of his lunchbox, but again, nothing was said.

———

ARTHUR TOOK deep calming breaths in his cubicle. It had been two weeks and the conversations had not gotten easier. He had managed to make a few minutes of small talk about the weather, a couple of sports teams, and the most recent Marvel movie which he'd finally managed to see. There were only a few lunch room regulars he hadn't introduced himself to yet, including the guy across the hall who always wore the exact same suit, got tea at the exact same time each day, as well as lunch, arrived and left on a clockwork schedule, and whom Arthur had never seen utter a single word to anyone.

A particularly tricky request had dropped into his inbox that morning and made him later than usual when he stepped into the lunch room. It was Monday, which was always the most crowded. There were only two seats free. One across from the man in the dark grey suit and the other across from a blond woman with a pageboy bob, he hadn't met yet.

"Hi, could I-"

"Lesbian." The woman didn't even look up from her yogurt.

"What?"

"You've spent the last two weeks flashing a charming smile and looking over everyone here. Lesbian, you don't stand a chance, so don't bother."

Arthur blinked at her. He was pretty sure he'd never been called charming by anyone ever and it never remotely occurred to him that what he was doing might be coming across as anything other than awkwardly friendly. He blinked a few more times then took a deep breath and held out his hand.

"Hi, Arthur Drams, level two analyst, trying, badly apparently, to make friends because I'm really tired of getting promoted sideways because my own supervisors forget I exist."

The woman looked him up and down, then briefly shook his hand.

"Carol. Sit."

Arthur sat and, for the first time since he got to the fifth floor, felt relaxed.

"How long have you been level two?" She asked

"Four years on three different floors."

"Ouch."

"My last supervisor told me he had to look up my picture to figure out who'd submitted the promotion paperwork. He told me I should try to be more social."

Carol winced. "Hate to tell you, but it's coming across less social and more... creepy. But you're also obviously uncomfortable enough to make other people feel uncomfortable."

Arthur put his face in his hand. "Fuck my life," he muttered.

Carol gave a small snort of laughter. He sighed and opened up his lunch box.

"And for a white guy, your lunches are almost exclusively Vietnamese food. Nothing wrong with that, but it's noticeable."

"I semi grew up in a Vietnamese restaurant kitchen. It's what I know how to cook best. It's complicated."

"Looks good though."

He looked at her single yogurt and held out half his bánh mì sandwich.

She smiled "Don't mind if I do."

———

THE NEXT day Arthur got to the lunchroom early and looked for Carol. She wasn't there and everyone else was looking away. He sat by himself. It was a horrible rehashing of high school, but he hoped that he would come across less weird. Or at least less creepy weird.

Hopefully, Carol would tell other people that the new guy wasn't creepy, just really unused to being social.

A few days later Carol was in the lunch room again and let him sit with her. She seemed to take lunch at random times on random days, but it was nice to have someone actually willing to talk to him, even if it was only for a half hour a couple times a week.

He'd been on the fifth floor a little over a month when there was a lull in the conversation. "Okay, what's up with the guy who's always in the dark gray suit?" It had been niggling at him since day one.

Carol didn't look over her shoulder like most people would. "You mean the Alien?"

Arthur didn't answer. He couldn't help but be aware of the dark suited man who sat across from him. His habits were clockwork. 8:05 at his desk, 10:00 a.m. cup of tea, 12:30 lunch, 3:00 p.m. cup of tea, 5:30 leave.

"Our best guess is that he crashed at Roswell and, after poking and prodding, they couldn't decide what to do with him so they gave him a human face and sent him here. He eats exactly one apple at the same time every day and is always reading books no one would read for fun. Three years, I've seen him talk to exactly no one."

"Has anyone talked to him?"

Carol looked over her shoulder. "A copy of *The History of the Peloponnesian War, Volume 3* is a pretty good Go Away sign in my experience."

Arthur looked over at The Alien. It was a Go Away sign, but it was a very specific type of go away sign; it was the kind that said 'Look at Me Just for A Moment. I'm Weird. If you talk to me you're going to decide I'm weird and not like me so let's just save both of us the public discomfort of you feeling the need to reject me.' He'd used that same trick in high school with copies of The Prince and Art of War. There might have also been some eyeliner involved. He could also remember being desperately lonely and wanting someone else's weirdness to match with his.

———

FOR ANOTHER month Arthur watched the Gray Suited Man, wondering if their weirdness just might match.

He was late to the lunch room when he had his first chance to find out. It was the first Monday of the month when everyone decided they were going to start packing their own healthy lunches. By Friday, half of them would be getting pizza in the cafeteria.

There was only one seat left in the room.

"Hi, can I sit here?" He was mostly addressing a copy of *The History of Foreign Investment in the United States, 1914-1945*. The Gray Suited Man raised his head and nodded slightly.

Arthur held out his hand as he sat. "Arthur–"

"Drams. Twenty-Nine, Analyst Level Two. Three illegitimate half-sisters. Bachelors in Social Anthropology, Masters in World Economies. Conversational Spanish, French and Vietnamese, though heavily accented and the French is dated as to be useless to the Agency. Certificate in Portuguese, both European and Brazilian varieties."

Arthur blinked once. The Gray Suited Man was obviously not a fellow level two analyst if he had access to Arthur's personnel file. Then there was the fact that he'd looked it up and memorized the salient points. That was an impressive step in the 'I'm Weird so don't bother acknowledging my existence' game.

"I also enjoy classic Film Noir and have read every Robert Asprin book. Even the bad ones where he was phoning it in."

The Gray Suited Man tipped his head to the side ever so slightly. Arthur didn't break eye contact, his hand still held out. He was being sized up. He wondered if those two bits of volunteered information would end up in his personnel file.

"And you are?"

There was a long five seconds of silence. "Martin Grove." He didn't shake hands, instead went back to his book.

Arthur opened his lunch and smiled with a small victory.

———

A FIFTH cup of coffee was calling to Arthur when he ran into Carol. Having language certificates in Portuguese, instead of the more currently useful Middle Eastern or Eastern European languages, meant any given week he had either stacks of work or virtually none. Somewhere in Brazil, some shit was going down big enough that some field agents felt the need to send actual information back to the main office. He had been up late writing briefing reports and it would be another late night as well.

"You talked to the Alien?" Carol whispered just outside the small breakroom that held the holy coffee machine.

It took a moment for his brain to process that question. "His name is Martin."

"And?"

"And that's more than a lunch room full of secret agents has bothered to get in several years."

"We're not secret agents. We're data management. If we were secret agents, I'd have a much cooler car and have much hotter women trying to sleep with me."

Arthur couldn't argue with that one. "You could try talking with him yourself."

"Nah. You've already got your foot in that door. And in case you're wondering, that stunt has gotten you noticed."

––––––––

IT WAS another week before Arthur managed to talk with Martin again. He slid into the seat across from him without asking this time. Martin briefly glanced up from his book, *One Quarter of Humanity: Malthusian Mythology and Chinese Realities, 1700-2000.*

"I read that as an undergrad. Retrospectively, I'm not sure if I entirely agree with it, but I've never encountered a sociology book that wasn't fairly heavily biased one way or another."

"The specificities of the author's bias is in itself a valuable path of analyses."

"That is true. Though at nineteen I was mostly annoyed that I couldn't sell it back at the end of the semester." He opened his lunch box. He'd made himself summer rolls but added in an extra.

No one could subsist on tea and a single apple. "Summer roll," he offered.

"No, thank you," Martin replied then went back to his book.

Arthur quietly crowed to himself. Two whole sentences. That was practically a conversation.

He fell into a sort of a rough pattern after that. Sometimes eating with Carol where they would talk about weather, sports, or if the ficus trees were real (she wasn't sure either). Other days he would eat with Martin.

It would often be in silence, but Martin never told him to leave. On 'conversation' days he could get maybe four sentences back and forth (not counting offers of food), on whatever Martin was reading at the time.

On the silent days, Arthur observed. The thing he observed most was just how fast Martin read. He always appeared to be idly flipping through books but he never had the same book twice and the way his eyes flicked led Arthur to believe he was reading every word. One day he watched Martin eat his six apple slices while getting two thirds of the way through *The Idea of the Good in Platonic-Aristotelian Philosophy.*

At that rate, he could understand why people called him The Alien. Arthur wasn't a slow reader, but he couldn't go at that speed. And there was something about the way he read. His eyes would be focused on the text, but he didn't hunch his back or drop his head in the slightest. His posture was perfectly straight without being stiff, more like a dancer than a soldier.

His fingers were long and his hands thin. Arthur would have sworn that pages of a book couldn't be turned gracefully, but Martin managed it. At one, without looking at a watch or clock, he would close his book, throw away the wax paper sandwich bag he carried his apple slices in, on a 'conversation day' possibly give Arthur the slightest of nods, then return to his empty cubicle across from Arthur's.

CHAPTER THREE

THERE WAS an itch right between Arthur's shoulder blades that he couldn't scratch because it was a mental itch instead of a physical one.

Martin's cubicle was empty and not in an arrived-early-then-went-off-for-meetings kind of way. Martin hadn't been in at all. There were subtle things he hadn't noticed when he walked into the wrong cubicle his first day on the floor, but everything about Martin was subtle. Now he noticed the way the Ethernet cable was still coiled away. His chair was tucked against his desk, the way he did when he left for the night as opposed to getting up for a cup of tea.

Martin's rigid schedule and habits had worked their way into Arthur's mind and the sudden lack of them was bugging him. He drummed his nails on the plastic mouse and contemplated asking his supervisor about Martin, except that wasn't the kind of thing you did in the Agency. People got promoted, demoted, shifted, fired and no one says a word. They are just there, then gone.

He glanced at the clock on the corner of his screen. It was after noon, but he didn't feel like eating. The discomfort at lack of routine was falling into worry.

"Fuck it."

He locked down his computer and decided he needed to get out of the building. He'd pop across the street and get something fast and fried for lunch. It would be nasty, but at least get him some non-recycled air and a bit of sunshine.

———

HE STROLLED through the parking garage instead of going through the front door. He got less of a hairy eyeball about going out for lunch from the parking guards than the ones at the front desk. He strolled up the row where Martin usually parked. He'd discovered it completely by accident and only remembered because the most immature part of his brain had snickered a little at it being spot 69.

A car was in the spot and that little tangle of worry that had been building over the morning spiked. He took a few long steps towards it then ran as he saw Martin slumped against the driver's side window.

"Hey!" he shouted banging on the window and testing the door handle. "Martin!" he yelled louder pounding harder on the window. He jiggled the handle a bit more, hoping to set off some sort of alarm. Still banging on the window with one hand, he checked his phone but he knew there would be no signal to call security and he had nothing on him that could break car window glass.

"Help!" He yelled as loud as he could, hoping his voice might echo through the large underground lot getting someone's attention. "Help!" He heard a car coming down the row and rushed to jump in front of it. The driver slammed on the breaks and rolled down his window.

"Get an ambulance and security. Someone is passed out in their car, I can't tell if they're breathing." He didn't wait for acknowledgment from the driver but did hear the car speed off as he ran back to Martin's spot.

He tried all the other doors knowing in his heart they would be locked. He pounded on the window some more. "Come on. Just move. Come on."

Security arrived first. The guard looked over the situation and with one quick movement, shattered the back-seat window with a small pointed hammer. It took a few more seconds to knock away the safety glass, the car alarm blaring, before he reached around and unlocked the door. Arthur yanked it open and Martin fell out into his arms. He was burning up. He coughed once and a fine mist of blood covered Arthur's face.

———

AFTER THE initial panic subsided, quarantine was incredibly boring. Arthur wasn't sure how long he'd been in the quarantine unit in the sub-basement of Central Hospital. Probably hours, but it was feeling like days. They'd taken everything off him, a good deal of blood out of him, and hosed him down. He was chilly in his paper dress and tired of the beep of the monitoring systems he was hooked up to.

The airlock door hissed open and a doctor walked in, free of all the quarantine equipment. "Agent Drams?"

"Yes?"

"You are free to go. I'll have a nurse bring your pants." The doctor turned to leave.

"Wait, what, I'm fine?" Arthur heard his heart rate speed up and took the monitor off his finger.

"You are perfectly healthy. Actually, good odds you'll come down with the flu in the next couple of weeks. Drink plenty of fluids, get some rest, take Tylenol if the fever gets above a hundred." The doctor made to leave again.

"Wait, that was the flu? Martin just has the flu? He coughed blood on me."

"I can't discuss another patient."

"Can I see him?"

The doctor looked tired, annoyed, and like he was about to simply walk out. Arthur thought as fast as he could. He'd spent a good deal of his life lying to important people about one thing or another. He was good. He stepped up close to the doctor and lowered his voice. "Look, Agent Grove and I are... involved. Just recent. It's against office policy but... Can I just, I just want to know if he's okay. Please?" He tried putting on sad puppy eyes but didn't know if it would work on doctors.

The doctor sighed. "He has the flu. He passed out in his car, ran a very high fever, had a bloody nose which dripped into his lungs, which is why you got covered in blood when he coughed. We're keeping him until tomorrow evening to make sure there's no complications from the fever and to get a vitamin drip and three meals in him."

"Vitamin drip?"

The doctor looked him up and down. "I'll take a guess you haven't made it past second base. Go out for dinner more often. He's about twenty pounds down on where he should be, but not so bad I can keep him here."

Arthur made the decision right then and there that he was going to be a little more insistent about lunch. "Okay. Absolutely."

The doctor gave a little huff. "Try to make him take a couple of days off work. Plenty of fluids and rest. He's on the seventh floor. I'll tell the nurses you're coming up."

"Thank you."

———

IT WAS another hour before Arthur got his pants back and managed to get out of the labyrinth that was the quarantine unit and into the main hospital lobby. It was nine and the gift shop was closed or he would have gotten Martin a book. From there he managed to find the seventh-floor nurses station.

"Hi, I'm here to see Agent Grove."

The nurse looked over her shoulder at the large clock on the wall then leveled a hard look at him.

"I'll just peek in really quick and if he's asleep I'll leave right away. Please."

"Room fifteen." Her voice was flat and she went right back to her charts.

"Thank you."

He peeked through the window of room 15. There was only one bed, but he couldn't tell if Martin was awake.

Slowly he pushed open the door, trying to be as quiet as possible. He wasn't sure if he woke up Martin or if he was already awake, but his eyes were open as he crept in.

"Hi," Arthur said, trying to keep his voice low. Martin's complexion was sallow and his hair matted with dried sweat. An IV ran into his arm. It was the first time Arthur had ever seen him without a suit on. His wrists were obviously thin and his collar bones prominent.

"I was told my boyfriend would be coming to visit."

Arthur's stomach dropped. "I had to think up something and I didn't think the doctor was going to believe 'It's a Matter of National Security' for the flu. Sorry."

Martin just nodded slightly. The silence hung a little too long.

What the fuck are you doing here? Arthur yelled at himself. *Just because you sometimes eat lunch with the guy, you think he wants you standing in his hospital room? He's probably got family or something that is going to check him out tomorrow.*

"I'm told you saved my life."

Arthur shrugged. "I was just walking by and saw you. It was security that broke open your car window."

Martin frowned slightly. "My window?"

"Yeah. Security had to break open the passenger window. I also think they might have pulled some wires to shut the alarm off."

Martin closed his eyes and let out a long sigh, seemingly sinking into himself. It was the most emotion Arthur had ever seen come from him.

"I can make some calls if you like, get the window fixed."

Martin shook his head. "I can handle it."

"I've been cleared, so is there anything you need? Anything I can bring you or someone I can call?"

Martin stared at him and he felt like he was being coldly analyzed.

"I have some library books that need to be returned by tomorrow."

"Sure."

Martin rolled over, reaching for his phone, wallet, and keys from the rolling hospital tray. Arthur saw his jaw tighten slightly as the IV line pulled but he didn't wince. He removed a key from the ring then a library card from his wallet and held them out. "The books are on my bedside table. I will send you my address."

Arthur squeezed the key tight, his heart speeding up. The man who talked to no one for three years and had probably spoken less than two hundred words to him had just handed him his house keys. It was a heady feeling.

"They need to be returned to the Erikson library on Eighth Street at exactly 11:55 tomorrow. They must be returned to the Special Collections desk. Tell the woman at the desk that they are from me. Do you understand all that?"

For the first time since joining the Agency, Arthur felt like he had a mission. What kind of library books required that much detail to return? "Erikson Library, 11:55, Special Collections."

"Thank you."

Arthur figured since he was being let into Martin's home he might as well push his luck a little further. "Do you have anyone picking you up tomorrow?"

Martin glanced away. "I will take a cab."

"I'll come get you. I have orders from your doctor to make sure you rest, eat, and take plenty of fluids."

"I will be perfectly well by tomorrow evening," Martin said as if he planned on glaring the flu germs into submission.

"You'll still need a lift home. I'll come get you."

————

IT WAS only when he got back down from the hospital room, still excited about receiving a mission, did he realize he needed a ride home as well. It was close to eleven when he finally made it home after an expensive cab ride back to the office. He checked his phone and noticed a strange little icon in the corner of the screen that he didn't recognize. He tapped it and the Agency messaging app came up and asked for a fingerprint. No one had ever sent him a message with the ultra-encrypted app, ever. He pushed his finger to the scanner on the back of the phone then scrambled to find a pen and paper before Martin's home address was automatically erased.

CHAPTER FOUR

THE ONLY word that could be used to describe Martin's apartment building was nondescript. Maybe utilitarian, if Arthur was being generous. The architectural brief had to have been 'make us a large box that we can put smaller boxes inside of. '

The key slid easily into the door of a small box on the third floor. He was expecting minimalism when he stepped in, but what he found was empty. He stepped back out to check the number and double check that yes, in fact, the key unlocked the door and it wasn't just that the door was unlocked already. There was a small table with a single chair next to the small kitchen area. The living room had no furniture. The cable for the television hookup was neatly coiled against the wall. There was a print of one of Toulouse Lautrec's Moulin Rouge cancan dancers, but other than that, not a shred of decoration.

It was eerie and Arthur was still wondering if he was in the right apartment. He could just find the bedroom and the library books, but instead he went to the kitchen. He knew that a kitchen could reveal more about a person than they knew. He opened the fridge and found it empty except for a bottle of milk. In the freezer, there was a box of single serve microwave frozen vegetables and single serve microwave chicken breasts. The cupboards had packets of single serve oatmeal.

No wonder he's underweight.

There was one glass. One tea cup of fine china, white with delicate blue flowers. One plate and one bowl with the same floral pattern. One fork, one knife, and one spoon, all of heavy silver.

He closed the last drawer, absolutely knowing that what he'd done was a violation of privacy and trust. He justified it as concern for Martin's health. Rightfully, so it would seem. It also creeped him out. Who has exactly one place setting and no more?

Someone who never plans on company.

The bedroom was easy to find. It was as barren as the rest of the place, the bed tightly made. With the amount Martin read, he had been expecting bookshelves. But the only books were the stack on the bedside table. All nonfiction, they ranged in topics and none of it light reading. He quickly gathered up the books and hurried out, the emptiness of the apartment beginning to feel like a physical presence, and an unfriendly one.

————

THE ERIKSON library had once been a grand building, gifted to the city by an early industrialist family so their name would live on. Now it was a large building that backed onto one of the most drug and crime ridden areas of the city, with bordering enclaves of recent immigrants trying to scrape together an American dream. The stained glass that survived had bars across it and the gilt paint had long since worn away. It was still the largest library in the city.

At 11:55 Arthur approached the Special Collections desk. An older woman with short cropped hair looked up at him.

"Yes?"

"Um, hi. Martin Grove sent me. He's sick and–"

"Oh, the poor dear." The librarian took the books from his arms and set them aside. "I was beginning to worry. He's never late. Will he be all right?"

"Yes, just got that flu that's going around."

The woman shook her head. "Probably got it from one of the kids. He loves them anyway." She stepped from behind the desk. "Well, come on, I'll show you to them. He's got them trained to all show up ten minutes early and get everything set up."

Arthur was confused, but had no doubt he'd just been volunteered for something against his will. He followed the librarian through the stacks until they opened up into an airy modern side building with lower shelves and bright colors. In a side corner, where he was being led, was what looked like a mini school area with some tables, chairs, white boards, and educational posters on the wall. A group of kids was sitting on the rug talking with each other.

"Hello children." The kids all looked up at the librarian. There were nearly twenty of them. Most of them looked to be maybe eight or nine. A few were older, maybe twelvish, a few might have been six or seven, but he wasn't practiced at guessing these things. They were bundled up against the cold outside and the cool inside and he was willing to guess that they were from the surrounding area. "Unfortunately, Merlin is sick today."

Merlin?

There was a small whine from the kids. "However, he sent someone else along today and I'm sure he'll be well and back next week."

The librarian gave Arthur a small nod, then left. He looked at the faces looking up at him. "Hi, um... I'm Arthur." There were quick excited whispers from the children.

"So..." he dragged out the word, not sure what he was supposed to do in the face of twenty children and the fact that The Alien was apparently the Saturday children's library storyteller. "Where are we?"

"We're at line 189, the start of section three," a little girl at the front volunteered.

"Okay." Arthur looked around. The girl got up, took a book from the shelf and handed it to him. "Beowulf. Okay." He could handle a little epic poetry and the children were all looking up at him with eager expressions. He opened the book. It wasn't in English. At least not any form of English he understood. He flipped through hoping to find a translation in the back or something, but there was nothing.

He closed the book again. "How does Mart- Merlin usually do this, because he didn't leave me any instructions?"

"He reads five lines, then presents us with a translation, and at the end we go over new words."

"Okay." Arthur opened the book then closed it again. "You know what, I wouldn't want to interrupt his flow so why don't we-" He looked around and spotted some crayons and construction paper. "Why don't we make some get well cards for Merlin."

The children each gave him cold stares. It was like being looked at by twenty tiny Martins. It was scary.

"Okay, I can't read this."

"Merlin hasn't taught you old English yet?"

"No, he hasn't. It's on the list. I can read you something else? We can make cards?"

"You didn't collect homework."

"He gives you homework?" Arthur had some memories of the local children's library growing up and he was pretty sure there was no homework or old English epic poetry involved. The children each pulled lined paper out of bags and passed them forward. He flicked through them. They seemed to be about the history of Beowulf, but what Arthur noticed the most was that all the papers, even from the youngest kids, were all in the most perfect of cursive letters. It reminded him of Hanh's elegant writing, which had been beaten into her by nuns.

"I will pass these on to him. I am sure they will cheer him up. Now how about those get-well cards and you all can start teaching me old English so maybe next time I'll be able to catch up.

———

IT WAS only an hour but Arthur felt absolutely drained when he leaned on the Special Collections desk, his arms full of essays and cards depicting the slaughter of mythical beasts.

"He didn't tell you that you would be doing story time, did he?"

"No. No, he didn't."

The librarian laughed. "No one ever said our Merlin didn't have a prankster streak in him."

"That is true," Arthur was forced to agree. "I don't recall story time as a kid involving Beowulf. At worst, I think we got *Bunnicula*."

"When our last reader didn't show up, we asked him to fill in. He thought the children were advanced students here for extra weekend study, not kids dumped here by their parents for an hour of free babysitting. Research has shown that if you treat children like they are advanced and gifted, they start acting like they are advanced and gifted, so why tell him otherwise. He pushes them, praises them, tells them they can do more than they think they can and, for him, they do."

"Okay. Merlin?"

The librarian put her hands up with a smile. "No idea where that came from but he doesn't seem to mind. He's going to be okay, right?"

"Just the flu. Didn't take care of himself when he should have."

"Silly boy," The librarian said with a fond smile and a shake of her head. Then she picked up a tall stack of books and placed them on the desk. "Here is this week's order."

Arthur sighed and pulled out Martin's library card. He wondered if he could get a bag.

———

ARTHUR HAD called the hospital to check when Martin was being released. He was still listed somewhere as boyfriend and it was a liberal enough hospital not to care. It was seven when he walked into Martin's room and found him tying his tie.

"Wes hāl," he greeted him with one of the dozen phrases the children had managed to teach him. "Seriously, you are going to walk out of here, on a Saturday, while still getting over the flu, wearing a suit."

"Yes." He adjusted his tie and picked up his coat.

Arthur held out a stack of paper. "Homework. Also, get well cards and a few drawings of Beowulf fighting off giant viruses which the kids drew because I can't read Old English!"

There was a tiny twitch to his lips. Arthur was pretty sure from anyone else he would be hearing hysterical laughter.

"Your books are all back at your place."

"Thank you."

"You're welcome, Merlin." Martin did not falter in the slightest at the name. "You know you could have just said 'by the way, would you mind reading to a bunch of kids for an hour'. You didn't have to completely troll me."

There was another tiny flick to Martin's lips. "True."

Arthur sighed. "Come on, let's get you home."

———

AT THE door to Martin's apartment he said thank you again and made to go in alone. Arthur ignored the signals and followed Martin in. He'd used the apartment key and the afternoon to make sure at least some of the doctor's advice was followed.

"I made you some dinner."

"You didn't have to do that," was Martin's instant reply.

"Doctor's orders. As your *boyfriend*, I am supposed to make sure you eat, drink some fluids, and get plenty of rest. So, go change, take a shower, whatever, and I'll heat up dinner."

Martin stared at him. It was a hard stare. It probably sent other agents and most people scurrying for their lives. Arthur had spent his childhood facing worse. Instead, he turned and strolled to the kitchen where he had set up before going to fetch Martin.

He'd heated the soup stock before going to the hospital so it was still warm and the meat and vegetables were precooked and in the fridge. All that was left was to warm up the stock a bit more and boil the noodles. It was at least a minute before he heard Martin's bedroom door open and close. A few minutes later he heard the shower run. He placed the shredded chicken and vegetables on the table. When the shower turned off, he ladled the stock and noodles into large bowls he'd brought from home along with a folding chair.

When Martin came out, he was in a white shirt and dress pants, but had removed his tie and jacket. He looked at the table.

"Do you know how to use chopsticks?" Arthur asked.

"No," he replied not taking his eyes off the food.

"No problem." Arthur put down the heavy silver forks next to the large white bowl. "This is Pho. National dish of Vietnam. Rice noodles in a special broth. Guaranteed to cure just about anything. Highly customizable. I like mine with raw beef, bean sprouts, and jalapenos but I don't think your system can handle that. So, for you, shredded chicken, your choice of vegetables and I recommend a squeeze of lemon.

"You didn't have to do this," Martin repeated, having not moved towards the table.

"Yes, I did." Arthur kept his voice firm. "You might do the scary man in almost black thing at work but you obviously don't cook or pay proper attention to your own health so I am going to stay right here until I witness you consuming some vegetables, carbs, and protein. You don't have to eat it all. You'd probably get sick if you tried, but you sweated yourself half to death then coughed blood on me, so you need to eat."

Martin continued to stare at the food.

"It's not Kæstur hákarl. Sit down and eat."

With slow steps Martin crossed the room and sat at his own table.

"That's better." When Martin made no other moves, Arthur placed a few slices of chicken on top of the noodles, a sprinkling of vegetables, then topped the whole thing with a squeeze of lemon. Then he held up a fork and a large spoon.

Apparently accepting a graceful defeat, Martin took the spoon and sipped at the warm broth. His face remained neutral but Arthur noted a slight flutter of his eyes. "There, that wasn't so bad, now was it?"

CHAPTER FIVE

ARTHUR WAS still riding his victory, as small as it was, on Monday. He had gotten Martin to drink at least a cup of broth, eat a few noodles, a couple of vegetables, and a piece of chicken. It was probably a higher caloric content then he'd had at any one given meal in who knows how long. What's more, he seemed to enjoy it, though he would probably be three days dead before admitting to it.

He left more and better food in Martin's fridge with a strong suggestion that he eat it on Sunday. He had no idea if that would happen, but at least he could say he got one meal into him.

He was in his cube at his regular time on Monday. He didn't stop to greet Arthur, but he never did. He didn't expect things at work to change just because he'd gotten a peek into Martin's life. That his brain was half fried by fever no doubt worked in Arthur's favor. However, Arthur was going to institute one small change into Martin's daily routine if he could manage it.

Arthur sat down across from Martin. He glanced at the day's book: *Coproduction and Coarticulation in IsiZulu Clicks*. He'd made summer rolls for his lunch. They were one of his favorite things. The crunch of mint leaves and lettuce, the chewiness of the rice noodles, the savory bite of sausage with the mildness of the shredded carrot. His were never as good as Hanh's, but they were not half bad.

Martin didn't acknowledge him as he sat but then he seldom did. He turned the page of his book, then picked one of his first of six apple slices. He did look a good deal healthier than he had on Saturday, but Arthur was close enough to see that his skin was still pale and he had rings around his eyes that hadn't been there before.

He had looked up the calories in an apple, and even a large one had barely a hundred. He took one of the summer rolls from his lunch. He'd made them half the usual size. No wider than a D sized battery and not much longer. He placed it where a single apple slice had been.

Martin showed no outward sign that he noticed the addition to his meal. His eyes continued to flick across the page. Arthur picked up his own and began to eat. He felt eyes on him from other parts of the room. It reminded him of high school. He'd solidified himself as one of the weird kids by trying to make friends with the really weird kid.

Martin ate his apple, one slice at a time, and read his book, the summer roll sitting ignored.

Arthur checked his watch. There was five minutes left in lunch, the six apple slices were gone, and Martin was nearing the end of his book. His eyes flicked up to Arthur for a split second, the first acknowledgment he'd gotten, then back down to the book.

"Chilled noodles, shredded carrot, fresh mint, and a small piece of *Goi Lua* sausage that I make myself. Nothing weird and you can't say you don't need it."

There was no acknowledgment. Arthur waited. He was good at waiting. Martin would either eat it or he wouldn't. Arthur wouldn't make a public scene either way. Wouldn't tell the office about Merlin or the hospital stay. He understood privacy and the need for secrets better than most.

He checked his watch. It was two minutes past one. Martin always ended his lunch at one, his internal clock perfect. He could chalk it up to lingering illness. Martin should probably still be at home in bed. He could attribute it to the fact that there were only a few more pages left in his book and he wanted to finish it but the way his eyes flicked across the page had slowed.

Then, with the same lack of interest that he picked up apple slices, he took the summer roll and ate it.

Arthur's heart raced. He wanted to smile but he kept his face as cool and disinterested as Martin kept his.

In three bites, just like the apple slices, the summer roll was finished and with no comment or even a nod, he finished his book and left. Arthur gave him a minute head start before packing up his lunch box and going back to his cube.

———

"YOU'RE FEEDING the Alien." Carol ambushed him in the break room as he was reaching for the coffee.

"His name is Martin."

"And you're feeding him."

"Someone has to."

Carol folded her arms and looked him up and down much the way she had the first day they met. "You were one of those kids who brought home stray dogs and tried to hide them from your parents even after they bit you."

Arthur poured his coffee, wondering if somehow she had seen the still ragged bit of scar tissue on his ankle.

"Just because a dog bites doesn't mean it's a bad dog."

"Doesn't change the fact that it bit you."

He shrugged slightly and stirred some sugar into his coffee wishing it was sweetened condensed milk.

"By the way, have you heard anything about the big bio-hazard lock-down last Friday?"

"Not really." He could play it as cool as anyone else. "Heard someone didn't get their flu shot and someone else overreacted."

Carol squinted at him. "Sure. Well, have fun. Don't get bit."

———

IT HAD been a long time since Arthur had anyone to cook for. Even then, most of that cooking had been done in Hanh's restaurant under the sharp eyes of his sisters before he left home for good.

He'd impressed a few guys and even a couple of girls in college by putting together non-instant meals using little more than a two-burner hotplate in his dorm room. But those relationships had never lasted long. He'd always had grand ideas of meetings of minds or souls, someone who fit grandly into the empty places of his heart, but that dream never materialized. The sex, what there was, always felt flat and mechanical, never spurring him on to something deeper.

There had been some dates, once he joined the Agency, but having to lie about his work put early strain on possible relationships before he ever got to 'come back to my place and let me cook.'

But now he had someone to cook for. Sort of. He had someone to bring very small portions of lite foods, during lunch, so whatever he made had to be small, portable, and maintain quality after sitting in a lunch box for five hours.

He made sandwiches, cut down to fancy party hors d'oeuvre size on Tuesday. He also brought his own book; *Walden and Civil Disobedience* which had been on his 'to read' list for a decade. On Wednesday, he pushed a little too far with a slice of sticky rice cake. Martin took a bite. There was a slight tightening around his eyes and he didn't finish the rest. Arthur supposed it was an acquired taste.

By Friday he was halfway through Walden, had probably gotten close to a thousand extra calories into Martin, along with fresh vitamins and minerals, and aside from telling him what each thing was, they hadn't spoken a word.

———

"IT'S LIKE a weird version of that scene in *Lady and the Tramp* where he's shoving the last meatball at her."

"I doubt he'd appreciate that analogy," Arthur told Carol as they both stirred their coffee.

"Unless you two spend an hour on the phone chatting each night, I doubt he's said more than two hundred words to you."

"There is more than one way to communicate," he stated, Carol hitting uncomfortably close to the truth.

"I'm sure there's a culture somewhere where silently shoving finger food at someone is an acceptable form of courting. Hobbits maybe."

"I'm not-"

"Yes, you are and it's adorable. Weird, but hey, I've got no room to talk, whatever floats your boat."

"I'm just bringing food for a friend who doesn't cook."

Carol patted him on the cheek. "Just keep telling yourself that."

———

ARTHUR SPENT Saturday morning shopping. And at noon, when Martin would be reading Beowulf to a group of school kids, he started making stock. It was a weird form of ignoring issues and he knew it. He had three large pots going on his stove, each slowly boiling down meats, vegetables, and herbs until he'd have a few dozen little jelly cubes flavored with beef, chicken, or fish to keep in his freezer.

He'd been a teenager before he hadn't needed a stool to see into the giant stockpots filled with cracked beef bones and chicken carcasses that had bubbled away on the restaurant's industrial stoves on Saturday mornings.

Not courting, feeding a friend, he told himself before calling up the sound of Hanh's voice telling him to focus.

Was Martin even really a friend? he asked himself while carefully skimming the fish stock to preserve clarity. But then he remembered Martin's apartment key. It was still on his key ring. He'd forgotten to leave it on Saturday and Martin hadn't asked for it back. That had to be a sign of friendship or at least trust. He had no doubt that if he told anyone about the kids at the library, not only would he demand his key back but probably also find some way of making Arthur disappear.

He turned the heat down on the chicken stock. He refused to

use the egg white method to clarify and sweating over large steaming pots was sort of what he needed.

————

MONDAY WAS sandwiches again and finishing *Walden*. Tuesday, Summer rolls and by Wednesday he dipped into his smaller but detailed French repertoire with Pissaladière, knowing anchovy paste would be a risk and probably not win him many friends in the lunch room. By Friday he was working on *The Wealth of Nations* and decided that it was definitely nice to have someone to cook for, even if the rest of the office thought they were weird. They were secret agents. They were all a bit weird.

————

IT WAS three weeks since the flu, which he'd managed to avoid getting, when he found Martin standing next to his car at the end of the day.

"The children have been asking after you."

"Really?"

"I think they were quite excited that your name is Arthur."

"Arthur to their Merlin."

"Yes."

There was silence in the parking lot. Martin's hands were neatly clasped behind his back and his chin was up.

"I'm not doing anything tomorrow." Arthur answered the question he thought Martin might be wanting to ask. "I could come by the library."

"I believe the children would enjoy that."

"Okay."

Martin gave him a slight nod and walked away. Arthur felt a little flutter, like he'd just been asked on a date.

CHAPTER SIX

AT 11:50, Arthur was, once again, in the children's section of the Erikson Library, watching a bunch of kids smile at Martin and Martin smile at them. He was in his suit and shined shoes, only the tie was missing.

"Everyone, you remember Arthur, who attempted to fill in while I was ill."

Most of the kids said hello. "He's not very good at reading," one of the youngest piped up.

"I have no doubt he will learn."

Arthur saw copies of Beowulf in his future. At least he'd have something to read during lunch.

"Your writings." The children passed forward their papers. "Last week's papers showed some interesting thoughts on Grendel's mother."

"It's understandable why she kills Æschere," One of the older children in the back of the group said.

"It is, and at some point, we will discuss themes of revenge and how it fits into historic writings and modern society."

Arthur was pretty sure he'd half slept through that lecture in philosophy 101, but the children looked interested. Martin picked up the copy of Beowulf that had left him floundering and began to read.

It was beautiful and hypnotic to listen to. Martin's voice gave the old English a musical quality and an easy rhythm to follow, which somehow managed to flow into his modern English translations. His fingers brushed along the lines as he read, but if Arthur had been told he was reciting it from memory he would not have been surprised.

At the end of sections, he would stop and ask the children their thoughts. They did not raise their hands, instead just put out whatever came to their minds. Only when it was obvious that a quieter child had something to say did he ask for silence from the rest.

When debate was finished, he would begin reading again, his face animated and the smiles easy, drawing Arthur in.

It was a jolt when he gave a final translation and closed the book.

"Hrothgar warns Beowulf of the risk of pride. Why? And why should or shouldn't he have pride in his victory. I want your thoughts next week."

The children nodded and began talking over each other, again throwing out ideas, arguments, and counter arguments but also listening to each other. At a time when a comment section on a cute kitten video could turn into a screaming match of slurs and threats of violence, it was the most hopeful thing he had ever seen.

Eventually the children quieted down.

"Perhaps Arthur would like to draw out the quote of the day?"

Martin held out what looked like an old tissue box decorated with popsicle sticks. He reached in and pulled out a slip of paper. "Do I contradict myself?" He read. "Very well then I contradict myself, (I am large, I contain multitudes.) Walt Whitman - Song of Myself. "

"American poet, born 1819, lived into his seventies. What does containing multitudes mean to you? We'll talk about it after Beowulf fights a dragon. Also, while in his seventies. See you next week."

The children got up, saying goodbye to Martin and Arthur before dispersing into the stacks. Possibly to look for works by Whitman.

Martin packed up the papers into a plain black shoulder bag, his face quickly losing the animation of just moments before though it had not yet reached the same hard stillness he showed at work.

"They all have impressive handwriting." Arthur commented, hoping for some conversation, something to keep Martin from pulling completely back into himself.

"A dying art that increases hand eye coordination and tran-shemispheric communication in the brain."

"So, which translation of Beowulf should I be working on so I don't completely embarrass myself in front of highly achieved seven year olds?"

"All of them. Begin with Seamus Heaney. That should be the most accessible for you." Martin didn't make eye contact and Arthur had a feeling he'd just had his intelligence insulted.

See if I don't just read all of them.

Arthur finished pushing in a few small chairs and followed Martin to the Special Collections desk, where a stack of books was waiting for him. They covered history, economics, and linguistics. There was no theme that Arthur could ever find. It was like Martin just played roulette with the nonfiction section of the library catalogue.

The librarian did take a moment to smile at him and say it was nice to see him again as she scanned Martin's books and handed them over.

"So," Arthur began before Martin could turn away. "I don't know if you have plans, but if you're willing to walk a few blocks through a questionable area I know of a good tea and dumpling shop? On me."

Martin's face had yet to retreat fully back into the silent blankness of work but it was headed that way. There was a flare of anger in Arthur's mind that he knew was irrational. It wasn't directed at Martin but at whatever it was, whatever happened, that made him feel he had to be The Alien around adults, but a smiling Merlin for the children. And he was certain Merlin was closer to his true self.

Eventually Martin gave a small nod. "Yes."

Arthur grinned and over Martin's shoulder he saw the librarian give him a smile and a wink.

———

MARTIN DROPPED his books off at his car then followed Arthur up the street. There were a few markets in the area where he got vegetables, spices, and cooking equipment that wasn't usually stocked at the local Safeway. The area was full of hole-in-the-wall restaurants where the majority of the menu wasn't in English and if you were white, the staff assumed you were lost.

The bell over the door rang and he waved at the waitress, who recognized him from previous visits. She pointed him to the only free table and brought over the menu that was just a long list of dumplings.

Do one thing and do it well.

Martin picked up his menu. Arthur thought he was getting pretty good at recognizing the subtle shifts and twitches around Martin's eyes and what they might mean. His eyebrows raised just a fraction as he read over the menu.

"The prawns with scallions are nice. Or the ones filled with cabbage?"

Martin nodded. There was a lot of information in those small, sharp nods.

He put down his menu. The waitress came over and he ordered a couple types of dumplings, tea, and two steamed milk buns. Mild but sweet and tasty. She looked to Martin who only slightly shook his head.

"Two plates," Arthur added.

A busboy left tea and two cups on the table. Arthur checked the tea and decided to let it steep. There was silence between them and for the first time in over a month, it felt slightly awkward.

"Merlin?" He finally asked, hoping to stir up a little conversation since they didn't have books to stick their noses in.

Martin looked away, his eyes scanning over the other patrons. "It did not occur to me that they could not read cursive when I wrote my name on the board. Their previous teacher had been reading stories of King Arthur."

Arthur grinned, picturing the situation. "They could make out an M, a tall letter in the middle and an N at the end and jumped to Merlin."

"They were quite excited about it."

"I can imagine."

Martin frowned slightly. "I fear a few of the youngest actually believe me to be Merlin."

"And having an Arthur show up didn't help that."

"No."

"There are worse people they could decide you are."

"That is true."

Arthur checked the tea again and, deciding it had steeped enough, poured two cups.

"What are you planning on after Beowulf?" Arthur asked, trying to keep the actual conversation going.

"I am considering returning to the Arthurian legends. *Le Morte d'Arthur* and *The Once and Future King* ostensibly tell the same stories, however, they present different underlying themes and messages. I may include sections of *Idylls of the King*."

"Good to know. That'll sort out my lunchtime reading."

Martin tipped his head slightly in a question.

"No, I haven't read them. My adolescent reading was mostly French poetry, science fiction I could get out of the school library, and a lot of bible study. *So* much bible study. Way too much bible study. And let me tell you, nothing gets you in trouble at Wednesday night Baptist bible study like quoting from the Epistle of Jeremiah." It was the only time he'd ever heard his mother raise her voice to his father and she had raised it high. He had already decided he was an atheist at that point and his mother's insistence on the *true* word of God and her screaming about Hanh ('That Woman' as his mother called her) and the Apocrypha was pointless. He took a sip of tea. "So, Beowulf then King Arthur. I think I can manage that."

Only after another sip of tea did he have the realization that he just invited himself to Saturday story time. Merlin did teach King Arthur and, while he doubted he'd ever be king of anything, there were worse ways of spending a Saturday than watching Martin's smiling animated face while he read works to small children that would floor most university graduates.

———

CAROL WAS grinning at him.

"What?"

She shrugged and kept grinning.

"What?" Arthur repeated.

Carol had become the closest thing he had to a 'normal' friend since shifting floors, mostly by teasing him during coffee breaks or giving him a warning when some major shit was rolling down the Agency. She'd developed her own sources and usually got a good five to ten minute warning before everyone was dragged into a conference room to be yelled at as a group, despite no one in the group actually doing anything wrong. For some reason, Martin was never in those meetings.

Arthur grabbed the coffeepot, giving Carol sideways glances. She was still grinning at him.

"What?" Arthur asked one more time.

"You're happy, so I'm making up random guesses and amusing little stories as to why."

"Don't you have more interesting things to think about?" Arthur asked trying to deflect the statement about his happiness.

"In case you haven't noticed, for a bunch of *secret agents* we have a really boring job. This passes the time. So, my best guess is you finally got a date out of mister Put-the-Secret-Into-Secret-Agent."

Arthur rolled his eyes.

"Aww, you did."

"No."

"You did too, or something close to it. I'm picturing either reading quietly in the library while casting little glances at each other or wild passionate sex. Okay, I'm not actively visualizing the sex because it's not my thing but, you know, it's always the quiet ones who get freaky behind closed doors."

"We didn't have a date. I'm not courting. It's just—" Arthur cut himself off, not having a good word for it and not wanting to dig himself into a hole with Carol. "Why do I like you, again?" he asked.

"Because I'm the only one here who doesn't think you're weird. Actually, I do think you're weird, but it's a workable weird."

"Well—" Arthur puffed himself up trying to mount some defense. "I think you're a little weird, too."

Carol grinned broadly at him, flashing her teeth. "Yes, I am."

CHAPTER SEVEN

THE THICK knot of worry in Arthur's stomach refused to ease. Martin wasn't at his desk. He hadn't been in all day. When he hadn't shown by tea, Arthur was going to pop downstairs and check his parking spot, except that's when a flood of work dropped into his inbox. There was a coup or something going down somewhere and the Agency was involved somehow, he was sure. It was one of the more frustrating parts of the job. It wasn't seeing puzzle pieces without the whole picture, it was only seeing individual close-up glimpses of a single piece. That didn't mean that those pieces didn't have to be analyzed right then and there.

He sent off his twelfth analysis for the day, then stood up to stretch his back. He peeked into Martin's cube, knowing full well it would be empty. All around he could hear fingers frantically flying over keyboards. He sat down and followed suit.

———

IT WAS 8:30 in the evening and he knocked on Martin's door for the third time. His car was in the building lot, so if he was somewhere else, he hadn't left by those means.

He knocked again. "It's me, it's Arthur, can you let me in? Or can you just come to the door so I know you're all right. I'm trying to not be weird and stalkerish about this, I'm really not." He pressed his ear to the door but only heard silence. "Okay, I'm going to let myself in just to make sure you didn't pass out in the shower and crack your head open. If you're fine, now is the time to tell me to screw off."

He waited and listened another minute before sliding the key into the lock.

"Hello?" he called out as he slowly pushed the door open. He heard nothing in return. "Hello?" A combination of panic and frustration began to build. He slid down the short entry hall and stopped. Sitting at the small table was Martin. From the back, he couldn't tell if he was breathing, or if it actually was Martin as he had seen far too many horror and noir films in his life. His heart was racing and he fought to keep his breathing steady.

"Martin?" He kept his voice soft as he slowly walked around the table. It *was* Martin sitting there. His eyes were open and Arthur could see the slight rise and fall of his chest. In the middle of the table was a fine china teacup and a large bottle of gin. The cap was on and the seal was in place. He leaned into Martin's field of vision. "Martin?" Martin's eyes flicked to his for a fraction of a second then went back to staring at the gin bottle.

Arthur let out a long and ragged breath, the worst of the panic receding back to general worry. "Okay, you're not dead on the floor of your shower. This is good."

Martin didn't acknowledge him. Arthur took a sniff. There was no smell of alcohol so he had probably just been staring at the bottle all day.

"I'm just going to take this and put it aside, okay?" He plucked the bottle off the table, receiving no objections, and put it in the kitchen. There was a black plastic bag, the kind distributed by liquor stores, and a receipt on the counter. He picked up the receipt. The time said 09:57. So Martin had gotten up, showered, dressed, possibly eaten his oatmeal, then something happened to get him to skip work, buy alcohol and then sit and stare at it for ten hours.

He was still staring at the place the bottle had been.

"Do you know it's after eight, at night?"

He didn't move for nearly a minute before giving a tiny shake of his head.

Nonverbal but responsive. I can work with this. Maybe.

"And I'll bet you haven't eaten, drunk, or possibly moved since sometime this morning."

This time it only took half a minute for Martin to shake his head.

"Do you want to talk about it?"

He got another head shake, this one almost instantaneous.

"Okay."

This was not a scenario he had planned for. He'd expected Martin to be missing, injured, or worst case, dead. He looked around the apartment trying to find anything else out of place, some clue as to what could be wrong, but everything was just as he'd seen it last time: barren, except for a print of a cancan dancer so out of place. He got up and walked over to it. The dancer, painted with red hair and a smiling face, her legs spread into the splits, was the only witness to anything that may have happened in the room.

As he stared at it some details came into focus. The thickness of the paper, the slight fading of the colors, the simple but careful framing. "Is this real?" He turned to Martin. "I mean, is this original? Like an original Lautrec."

Martin raised his head from the ghost of the gin bottle. "Yes." There was a rough scratch to his voice that Arthur had never heard.

"Wow. Where did you find it?"

"She was my great grandmother, many times over."

That pulled Arthur up short. He hadn't actually expected Martin to answer, and if he did, he wasn't expecting an answer like that. "She was very pretty."

"Yes." Martin had gone back to staring at nothing.

"Okay," Arthur clapped his hands together coming to a decision. "Due to my fondness for film noir, I know every retro, hipster movie theater in the area that serves good food and has late screenings. So, you are going to get up and I am going to take you someplace where you will eat, then sit in the dark and have the feelings you need to feel without engaging in alcohol poisoning or having people worrying that you slipped and died in your shower."

Martin blinked at him and, for possibly the first time, Arthur recognized confusion in his face.

"I'm serious. Your doctor told me you were twenty-five pounds underweight and you're not that tall. I will throw you over my shoulder and walk out of here," Arthur bluffed. He'd never been terribly strong in his upper body and would not be surprised if Martin could whip out super-secret ninja moves.

With a twitch of the lips, that might have been a smile, he began to stand only to crash back down to his chair. Arthur rushed to his side and slung an arm around him. "Easy. Let's try this again."

Martin leaned against his side and slowly pushed himself to his feet. His legs wobbled and he visibly winced. Arthur kept an arm low around his narrow waist as they took small steps around the table. He was still limping on both legs when he pulled himself from Arthur's side but didn't look to be at risk of falling over.

"Come on, grab your wallet and keys." Martin gave him a closed look like he was about to claim that he was fine, needed no assistance, and would send Arthur away. "Nope." Arthur preempted any argument. "Out the front door. Right now. Empty walls and gin are not healthy."

"You don't need to do this."

Arthur crossed his arms. He knew he didn't *need* to do this. For all of Carol's teasing and what he might have said to the doctor, Martin was still very much a mystery. He'd known more about the lives and background of casual acquaintances than he knew about Martin Grove, but those little slivers were something Arthur was coming to treasure. Not the information, but the trust that came with it. Martin might have been half delirious with fever when he first extended that trust, but he had done nothing to rescind it and Arthur had been careful to keep it.

"Your doctor didn't believe we were involved because I didn't know how thin you were. He wanted to hospitalize you but the best he could do was keep you overnight to get liquid vitamins into you, and I have no doubt you are smart enough to know that. Everyone needs someone to check in on them, even if it's just to make sure they haven't tripped and cracked their head open. And as much as you might want to argue with me, you know it to be true and necessary or you would have taken back your apartment key. You might be stubborn and scary and I've got no way of knowing what's really going on in your head, but you are in the amateur leagues compared to my sisters or my dad's mistress, and she can break a chicken down to pieces in under 20 seconds, and completely debone it in less than a minute. On a technical level, I don't need to do this but as a reasonably functional human who actually enjoys your company, yes I do."

Martin blinked at him. There were the same slight twitches around his eyes and mouth that had followed the first taste of that summer roll. It was well over a minute before his face settled back into stillness.

"Go get your wallet and your keys. We're going to go find a movie."

———

THE GLORIA Revival Theater had couches instead of seats and a second-rate sound system. What it also had was a quality kitchen and a 9:15 showing of *Gilda*. Not Arthur's all-time favorite of the genre, but not bad. Truthfully, it was way too late to be out when they both had work in the morning, but Martin needed to get *out* and Arthur wasn't about to take him clubbing.

He handed Martin a menu. "Pick something."

He hadn't said a word on the drive, only stared out the window. His eyes jumped over the menu, but he looked more confused than anything. How does someone, in American society, get to whatever miscellaneous age Martin might be, and seem totally perplexed by the simplest of menus? There was pizza listed. Yes, there were plenty of people who didn't, wouldn't, *couldn't* cook, but unless Martin had been raised in some secluded cult (a theory Arthur was willing to consider) he must have an opinion on pizza toppings. The lights blinked, announcing the start of the movie. Arthur sighed. "Antipasto plate for two and two chocolate milkshakes," he ordered.

The lights were left a little brighter than most theaters so people could see their food and drink. It also made it easier to see Martin. He kept his eyes on the screen, impassive at first, showing only his usual distance, but in the half-darkness his lips twitched into a smile when Rita Hayworth made her famous appearance with a grand toss of her hair.

And he ate, without prompting or pushing from Arthur. A full day with nothing was enough to break even *his* control. It wasn't much. A few cubes of cheese, a couple of olives, a little prosciutto, his face gaining animation as the film flickered on the screen.

Arthur knew there was a good chance he would never be told what had frozen up Martin that day, but with every little flicker of emotion, he felt better about his own actions that night.

Before the lights went up, Arthur was sure he saw a single tear slip from Martin's eyes. If a quirk of the lips was uproarious laughter, then that tear would have been heaving sobs on anyone else. He didn't comment, or acknowledge it, or make any intimation that he'd seen it at all.

———

MARTIN HADN'T spoken on the drive home any more than on the drive there. Arthur had been tempted to try to tuck him in, but he'd pushed the boundaries enough that night and Martin had opened up far more than he'd expected. Instead, he wished Martin a good night at the door and encouraged him to get some sleep.

Arthur went home and, instead of taking his own advice, stared at the ceiling over his bed. He was used to being entrusted with secrets beyond his job. His entire childhood had been keeping one giant secret, but it was a secret everyone knew. It was less keeping a secret and more not punching the kids who teased him about it. He'd also kept secrets about himself, but those were less deep and dark and more just not wanting to deal with the shit storm of acknowledging what everyone knew or at least suspected.

The secret of Martin was different. It lay quiet in his chest. It felt sacred, as if he had born witness to an ancient rite, rather than taking a depressed friend out for a movie. But the word 'friend' seemed not to fit. It was too vague and common. What he felt was more complicated than a word tossed about by children or achieved through a click of a mouse.

Maybe there was a word in old English, lost to modern ears. Martin let him see the cracks that night and the smallest hint of what lay beyond. He wanted to know what was truly beneath those cracks but also knew he would fight anyone who tried to break Martin open. For that feeling, he knew of no words.

Merlin and Arthur, Arthur and Merlin. Merlin appearing young yet wise, his lives flowing in reverse; but Arthur was no king past, future, or otherwise. Maybe one of those children who looked up at him with wide eyes and open minds had the making of a leader of legend. But not him.

He flipped over and yelled into his pillow. Becoming lunch buddies with the weird kid was not supposed to become this complicated, but not for one second did he feel like stopping.

———

ARTHUR MANAGED to drift for a few hours before his alarm went off. It hadn't helped. Instead, his mind had tossed up a recurring stress nightmare that had started when he was twelve. Walking into Hanh's kitchen and finding that none of the prep work had been done and his sisters weren't there and for some reason his eyes wouldn't focus so he couldn't read the order slips while he frantically tried to cook.

He woke up with a headache and a craving for really greasy pizza. He also woke up with a bit of an idea. Martin obviously had a first-class academic mind, but Arthur was no slouch and education did go both ways.

———

HE WASN'T surprised to see Martin at his desk working away. After all, the man had tried to drag himself into work half-dead with the flu. Arthur was tempted to pop his head in, to ask how he'd slept, how he was doing, but the office wasn't the place for that conversation, not between the two of them.

Martin got up for tea right on schedule and Arthur popped across the row. He'd had to dig around a few boxes of books that were never unpacked, but he finally found an old copy of *The Medieval Kitchen: Recipes from France and Italy*. Everyone should have an opinion on pizza toppings and he would drag Martin through the history of Italian cooking if he needed to.

CHAPTER EIGHT

ARTHUR DRUMMED his nails on the top of his mouse and wished his computer was properly hooked up to the Internet. He could get on, but the Agency blocked 90% of it and monitored the rest. He'd had two action items in his box when he arrived at work and he'd finished both of those by nine. All the weirdos, dictators, terrorists, and secret agents in the world and not one of them was doing a damn thing that needed his attention.

He checked the clock. It was still two hours until lunch. He was almost done with Tolkien's swing at Beowulf and had loaned Martin another couple of books on the sociology and history of food. They still didn't talk much, but since That Night the nature of the silence had changed, at least from Arthur's point of view. It felt more relaxed but heavier, like a warm blanket from the closet at the beginning of winter.

There was a buzz from inside his top desk drawer. The Agency would have preferred an absolutely no cell phone policy, but even they knew it was a losing battle. Instead, there were a stack of rules, tracking software, random checks, and phones had to be kept on vibrate in a desk drawer during business hours.

He pulled open the drawer with a hit of trepidation. No one called him. He flipped the phone over. 'Mom' flashed on the screen.

"Hello?" he said, tapping the green button. There was no reply.

"Hello?" he tried again. There was the sound of some gasping breath, then a sob.

"Arthur," his mother choked out.

"Mom, what is it?"

"Your... Your father—" She fell into tears and Arthur's heart froze. There were two things that could have happened: his father had left or his father was dead.

"Mom. Mom can you hand the phone to someone else? Is there someone there with you?"

His mother's sobs faded, then there was another voice on the line. "Hey, Arthur, it's Jennine."

"What happened?" he asked his mother's neighbor of many years.

She let out a long and heavy sigh. "I'm sorry Arthur but..." She trailed off.

"He's dead."

"Yes."

"Okay." Arthur felt his analytical mind start to disconnect from his emotions. He encouraged it. There was so much he was going to have to deal with due to his father's complicated life. He let the numb wave flow across him. He'd have time for emotions later. Right now, he had to be practical. It was going to suck.

"What happened?"

"He went out to get the paper and just collapsed, right there on the front walk. I saw him fall, called an ambulance, but they just couldn't get his heart going again."

"Okay. Where are you?"

"We're still at the hospital. There are all these people making your mother just sign paperwork."

"Okay." His mind was racing ahead. He had to get home, he had to plan a funeral because what his mom would want and what his dad would have wanted were two very different things. He had to call his sisters. "I'm going to get the first flight I can. Can you stay with my mom? Keep her... Yeah."

"Of course I can, dear. She'll be glad to have you home."

"Give her a hug for me and tell her I'll be home as soon as I can."

He tapped the disconnect on his phone then stared at it. His mind was running with all the things he needed to do but his body had frozen with the shock.

Step one, get out of here.

With a deep breath, he lurched to his feet and rushed to his supervisor's office. He knocked on the door and waited all of two seconds before popping his head in.

"Hi, I really need to talk to you."

Agent Collins looked around as if there might be someone else in the room. "Okay."

Arthur let himself all the way in but didn't sit down. "My dad just died. I need to take leave starting right now."

"HR has paper—"

"I don't have time for that. I need to be on the fastest flight out." His boss just raised his eyebrows at him. "Look, the last time my mom and my dad's mistress, whom he'd been with a couple of decades *before* meeting my mother, were in the same room, blood was spilled. My blood, in fact, when I tried to split them up. The cops were called, there were arrests, restraining orders, court mandated anger management, and I needed stitches. Throw my three half-sisters into this and I cannot explain how ugly this could get. I've got my mother's neighbor sitting on her but— "

"Okay, okay." Agent Collins cut him off. "Log into HR on your phone, fill out the paperwork and forward it to me by the end of the day and I'll pretend you're taking a half sick day right now."

"Thank you. You're the best supervisor here." That was step one checked off.

"No. I think I'm just the laziest. I like to deal with people's drama as little as possible. Paperwork before close of business."

"Promise."

"Are you still planning on organizing the Super Bowl pool?"

Arthur paused trying to follow the sudden leap in thought. "Yes. I'll set it up when I get back."

He rushed back down to his cubicle to gather stuff up. The required in-house Agency Wi-Fi would lock him out of any airline sales site. His best bet would be to drive right to the airport.

Go home and pack clothes first, a little voice in his head suggested.

Good idea.

He shoved his keys in his pocket preparing to sprint to the parking lot when he stopped and found himself staring at the back of Martin's head. He felt like he should say something. He'd twice criticized him for dropping off grid without notice and it would be hypocritical to suddenly not show up for lunch. He'd never spoken to Martin before at work outside of lunch or stepped foot in his cubicle since that first day.

"Hey," he finally said softly, wondering if Martin would even hear him. Martin swiveled in his chair, looking at Arthur with a tilt of his head. "My dad just died." It was strange to say that out loud.

Martin's eyes flicked back and forth as if he was reading down a list of appropriate responses. "I'm very sorry to hear that," he finally said.

"Yeah. I've got to get a flight. You can have my lunch, or give it to Carol. It's in the fridge."

Martin's eyes flicked again. "Thank you."

Arthur just nodded and left. He wasn't sure what exactly he had been expecting. Probably about what he got.

His mind continued to fill with a list of things he needed to do and fires he was going to have to put out and things he was going to have to organize. It was better than feeling. He didn't have time to break down. Sometime after the funeral he'd go out to his dad's old bar, put back a half dozen beers and cry a bit.

He was six blocks away from the office when he pulled over to make a call. He knew his calls were being monitored, recorded, and listened in on. He was low enough on the totem pole that he had no hope of privacy. His father's death was probably recorded in his file before he even knew about it.

He checked the time. Dinner prep would be on but lunch rush would be over. Not that Sonia was hands on in her kitchens anymore. She was running a little empire now, which got her out of peeling shrimp. It was still rude to call during rush.

The phone rang twice before she picked up.

"I know," she said before Arthur could even open his mouth. There was a flat efficiency in her voice.

"I wasn't sure."

"I'm still listed as a contact in his medical files."

"Does your mom know?" He couldn't imagine how Hanh might take the news.

"Yeah." Sonia didn't volunteer any more information.

"I'm getting the first flight out that I can."

"Your mother won't let us come and mom won't set foot in a Baptist church."

This was the nightmare scenario. The thing that made some small part of him hate his father, even in death. "I'll fix it. I'll make sure— " He wasn't sure. He had to. His father owed that to his sister and to Hanh but it would be up to him to make it happen.

"He was a bastard." Her voice was still flat.

"Yeah."

She finally sighed. "This is going to hurt when I finally let it."

"Yep. It really will. "

———

THE PLANE bumped to a landing and Arthur tried to unclench his hands from the armrests. He wasn't usually a nervous flyer, but there are only so many airlines that fly to small regional airports and are able to sell you a ticket on an hour's notice. For the most part, those airlines did not have the greatest safety record. The woman sitting next to him told him it was her commuter flight and she'd been doing it every week for a decade and they only had one emergency and that was before they even took off. Then she smiled at him in a way that made him unsure if she was a little crazy or just fucking with him. Either way, he'd spent the flight trying to quietly recite all the words in Old English he'd learned.

It was another twenty minutes before one of the airport's four gates had an opening. He was already on his phone by then, looking up funeral homes, flowers, and if the VA hall was free to hold the funeral. It's what his dad would have wanted even if his mother was going to throw a fit. He'd never been so glad for the simple google search "how to organize a funeral." There were checklists available.

It wasn't until the taxi drove past the Silver Oak Estates sign, painted orange by the low winter sun, that it started to hit, like a brick slammed into his chest. He took long deep breaths, trying to push it all back down. He was home. He'd go up the two brick steps, put his key in the lock, and his father wouldn't be there. Not to greet him. Not to offer him a beer. Not to run interference between him and his mother. He took a few long deep breaths and tried to think *what would Martin do?* That didn't help, as he'd been coming to the conclusion that Martin was a great swirling beast of emotion underneath the frozen alien exterior.

What would Spock do? Nope, no good either. Probably nerve pinch his mother out of frustration that he'd refuse to admit to.

"You okay?" the cabbie asked. He must have been muttering to himself or something weird.

"Yeah. My dad just died." It was the second time he'd said that and it still sounded strange. "And my mom is a bit nuts."

"Sorry to hear that."

"Thanks."

There were no more comments for the rest of the short drive. He handed over cash for the fare without waiting for change. He ran his fingers over the keys in his pocket as he approached the door. There was only one with a little rubber key cover that had dried and cracked over the years. Next to it was a simple key that opened the door to a barren apartment decorated only by a cancan dancer.

The key to his childhood home slipped easily into the lock. He pushed the door open slowly. The living room was full of older women in church pastels and the air was thick with a combination of perfume and casseroles.

His mother jumped up and ran to him. Her eyes were red, but at some point she must have redone her makeup. She never looked anything but proper in front of company. "Artie."

"Hi, Mom." He pulled her into a hug and she tucked her face into his shoulder. He squeezed her tight and felt her shake but beat his own emotions down hard.

Not yet.

She yanked herself away and brushed at his jacket. "Oh, I've smudged your coat."

"It's okay." He pulled her into another hug which she eventually left far more slowly. "How are you doing?"

She took a tissue from her pocket and dabbed carefully at the corner of her eyes, avoiding any more smudging of makeup. It always amazed him how much of her habits and simple mannerisms seemed to come from a completely different era. "Oh, you know. Not sure it's properly hit yet."

"I know the feeling."

She brushed at his shoulder again. "Why don't you put your bag in your room then come into the parlor." It was always the parlor. Not a living room or family room. Again, a holdover from an age she was never a part of.

"Sure."

His room was now one of two guest rooms, the posters and dented furniture long gone and replaced with tidy end tables and doilies.

He dropped his bag in the middle of the bed but was careful not to sit. He knew if he did, he wouldn't want to get up. He'd just sit there staring at the embroidered psalm hanging on the wall.

"Fuck you, Dad," he said quietly to the room. It was that last time he'd be able to cuss in the house.

When he got back out to the parlor, his mother instantly jumped up. "Oh dear, I didn't ask, did you eat on the plane? You should at least have some coffee."

"I'm fine Mom, really."

"Oh, it's no bother, Mary DeMill brought by a lovely quiche." She bustled into the kitchen before he could remind her that he hated quiche even though he could cook a damn good one.

He looked around at the other women. He knew most of them. They were as much into Jesus, not cussing, and behaving properly as his mother was, but were a little more practical about it. "How's she really doing?" he asked the room at large.

"Trying to keep busy, but better now that you're here," Jennine answered.

"Has she made any plans yet?"

"Not yet."

"Good." There would be less fighting if he could just make the plans instead of unmaking ones his dad would have hated. He'd read that funerals are more for the living than the dead, but the living involved would prove a complication.

His mother came back out with a slice of quiche on the good china, the stuff that only ever came out for Christmas and Easter.

"Sit down, Mom." He took the quiche, which had pulled away from the crust and looked to be filled with overcooked bell pepper and undercooked ham.

Don't be a food snob, he reminded himself.

"So, how is your work going?" One of his mother's friends asked. Looked like it was his turn to hold up the awkward conversation.

"Fine, not much new. Spend my day processing paperwork, really."

"Insurance, right?"

"Yep." That seemed to be the go to lie for half the Agency. "For international shipping."

"That's interesting." It was a full lie, but these were women with Master's degrees in making Polite Conversation under any circumstances.

"Not really. Get a big enough storm and those big shipping containers can fall off the side of a ship, then someone files a claim for 40,000 rubber ducks, or 200 computers, or whatever was in it."

"Does that happen often?"

"About 10,000 a year." He'd read an article about it a while back. "In the early 90's, 28,000 rubber ducks got lost in the middle of the Pacific, they're still washing ashore."

"How fascinating."

Arthur nodded and shoved a forkful of sub-par quiche into his mouth. He knew about twenty minute's worth of factoids on international shipping. He had to ration them.

"My Johnny's in life insurance. Doing quite well for himself," one of the pastel clad women said. And there was the start of the passive aggressive 'my son is doing better in business than yours' and 'my daughter has squeezed out more grandchildren for me than yours' competition. He knew from experience that his mother's good silver forks weren't sharp enough to drive through his own skull to make it stop.

While the ladies gossiped, Arthur choked down three more bites, which was what was required to be polite. There was a knock at the door and his mother jumped up before anyone else could. He was sure that over the next few days there would be a steady stream of church ladies stopping by to lend support, as well as quiches and casseroles. Somewhere along the line there would be a Jell-O mold, but those take a bit of time to set up.

"Arthur."

He turned around to answer his mother but anything he might have said just froze up in his head because Martin was standing next to his mother. Sort of. The man standing there more or less had Martin's face but he was dressed like Mr. Rogers and had a polite sympathetic smile.

"Martin?"

"It's so nice, your friend coming all the way here to help out."

"Uhhh..." All brain functions that might have been used to form words had shorted out.

"When I heard what happened I just had to." Martin's voice was sweet, modulated with just the right level of sympathy. "He was so helpful to me not that long ago and my job is mostly organizing complicated events on short notice. So really, Mrs. Drams, anything I can do to make this difficult time easier for you."

"Aren't you just the nicest young man." Arthur felt his eye twitch at his mother's words. "Would you like some coffee?"

"Oh, please, Mrs. Drams, allow me." Arthur watched as Martin took his mother's hands and led her back to her seat on the couch. It was like watching community theater. Martin's movements were just a little too stiff, his smile not quite right. Close. It was good acting if you didn't actually know Martin, but it wasn't winning any Oscars.

Arthur got up. "Martin. Why don't you help me get everyone more cake?" He didn't know if there was cake but he was willing to make a guess.

Once they got to the kitchen, he looked Martin up and down. "First, you're dressed like Mr. Rogers and it's freaking me out."

Martin tilted his head slightly. "Don't tell me you don't know who Mr. Rogers is because I *will* start telling people you're an alien. Second, you showing up here is a little on the creepy side but I pretended to be your boyfriend to acquire confidential medical information so I don't have a leg to stand on here. Third, what are you doing here?"

Martin's face settled into a more familiar one. The one he wore in dumpling shops and Mexican bakeries on Saturday afternoons. "I have a strong skill set in organizing complicated events involving people with disparate personalities on little notice. From what is listed in your personnel file, I thought you could use the assistance."

There was a flash of anger at Martin's assumptions, that he wouldn't be able to handle the coming disaster, that his father's fucking around would only lead to some public display for the ladies to gossip about for years. He was angrier at the fact that Martin was right. He was going to need at least one person on his side because everyone would assume he was on the other.

"Thank you."

———

IT WAS a few more hours before the last of the ladies cleared out. Not that Arthur payed much attention. The whole time he was watching Martin work on his audition for the role of Normal Human. Not that anyone else noticed, though. Martin fetched coffee and cake and made polite conversation and they all just thought he was the nicest young man they had ever met. Only when he was asked about his own family did he pause for a moment as if he was quickly reading down a script trying to figure out where he was in the show. Arthur wasn't sure what hurt more, the idea that what Martin said were lies or the truth. He had parents in Des Moines, he said, and a younger sister who was a nurse and just had her second child, a little girl this time and he was sorry he didn't have pictures, but Arthur had a feeling that by morning Martin could produce a whole phone full of happy family photos out of thin air.

They reheated one of the better-looking casseroles for dinner. He wanted to cook. It relaxed him and helped him think, but he knew it would just upset his mother. What he was planning on doing tomorrow would be bad enough.

Only once the dishes were washed (Martin insisted) and his mother was sent to bed, insisting Martin take the other guest room, did Arthur collapse onto the sofa and actually curl into a ball. Martin stood over him.

"Please tell me you brought your suits because, honestly, the zip up knitted sweater is a weird, weird look for you."

Martin's lips quirked up. "Yes."

"Oh, good. I wonder if my mom has already dumped my dad's stash of gin. Probably. Probably the first thing she did. Demon gin." Arthur slowly sat himself back up. "We need to have the funeral as soon as possible. Mom is going to want it in the church. Dad refused to set foot there; he always said he wanted it at the VA hall. There will be two big battles and that will be the first."

"And what will be the second?"

"Hanh." Arthur leaned forward pressing the heels of his hands to his forehead. "Some guys try to smuggle their service weapons out of the army. My dad smuggled out his seventeen-year-old French Vietnamese mistress. Brought her home, used his inheritance to set up her house, then help her set up a little noodle shop. Three-seater place. She wouldn't marry him for reasons I don't know. They had three kids. Every so often they'd have a fight, she'd chuck him out of the house for six months to a year. Last time that happened, he went to a bar and met a pretty young thing who was trying to bring drunks to Jesus and my father's a charming-as-fuck fucker. He was 45, mom was 25 and there was actually a shotgun present at the wedding. I've seen the pictures." Arthur flopped back and stared at the ceiling. "Every Friday evening my mother would leave dinner in the freezer and get into her car to spend the weekend spreading the good word of the lord out in the wilderness. Once she was at the end of the block, dad would put me in the car and we'd drive across the county line. My youngest sister, who's eight years older than me, hated me because she felt I was the reason daddy didn't come home. Hanh put me to work in the kitchen with my sisters by the time I was five and... My mother may be a bit ditzy at times but there was no way she didn't know what was going on. Fucking everyone in town knew what was going on. It has to be at the VA hall because Hanh and my sisters deserve to be there and Hanh is Catholic and hates my mother and won't step foot in a Baptist church and my mother would throw a fit and never let her in anyway. And frankly, my father loathed going to any kind of church and the first, last, and only time my mother and Hanh were in the same room together I ended up needing stitches trying to break up the fight." Arthur rolled his head to look at Martin, who hadn't moved. "And you can put all that in my personnel file if you like."

"No need."

"Yeah, probably all there already."

"I am very good at organizing difficult events on short notice."

"This one might be your masterpiece."

CHAPTER NINE

IT WAS a headache that woke Arthur, like a hangover without the fun of having been drunk. His mother had been thrifty with the guest sheets and it felt like he was rolling in sand. It was bright beyond the cracks in his curtains so it must have been late. He remembered turning off his work alarm before collapsing into bed but he must have forgotten to set another.

He could smell bacon though. His mother was not a spectacular cook but she could fry up a pan of bacon with the best of them. He stumbled out of bed, pulling on sweats and a t-shirt and followed his nose. Beyond the smell of bacon there was the sharp bite of cleaning chemicals and the burn of dust pulled through a vacuum cleaner.

He stepped into the parlor and found it was clean. His mother always kept a clean house but this was *clean*. Every inch of furniture looked freshly polished. The rug was vacuumed in such a way that the carpet fibers were all going the same direction. The coffee table books were stacked and dead center. Pictures straightened. The best picture of his father, hardly twenty in his dress uniform, was on the sideboard and bracketed by flowers that had been brought over.

The dining room was polished to a high gloss with the good china set to receive the visitors who would probably start dropping by soon.

He first came across what might loosely be considered a mess when he found a couple of rinsed breakfast dishes that had not yet been put into the washer. Martin and his mother were at the breakfast table in front of a laptop. Martin was thankfully back in a work shirt. He pointed to something on the screen and his mother nodded then looked up.

"Good morning, sleepy head." She smiled at him. It wasn't beaming and bright, but it didn't seem forced.

"Yeah, sorry, I forgot to set my alarm or something."

"Travel is always rough on the system. Get some coffee and have some breakfast." There was an empty setting at the table along with toast and bacon.

"Yeah." He grabbed a cup of coffee from the old pot and sat down across from his mother and Martin, still trying to shake the sleep from his head. "How long have you two been up?" He asked sliding some bacon onto this plate.

"Oh, just a couple of hours, but Martin here was already awake and I've never seen the house so clean."

Martin smiled. "It was really just a little dusting. I'm an early riser."

With anyone else at any other time Arthur might have made a crude joke at that last bit but instead he just sipped his coffee. His mother sighed.

"I know this is all so difficult, but I've decided to hold the funeral at the VA hall instead of the church. Your father would have wanted it that way and the church didn't have a free space open for two weeks. And I just feel it's for the best."

Arthur flicked his gaze to Martin whose face was masked off and unreadable. He had little doubt that his mother's decision was Martin talking her into it but making it feel like it was her idea. He could kiss the man. Instead he nodded solemnly. "Dad always did feel comfortable there."

"We have an appointment with the funeral home first thing tomorrow morning to pick out a coffin and all those other things. It's..." His mother let out a long sigh. "I feel horrible saying this, but this is all so inconvenient. Having to take time off work and all these little fiddly decisions."

There was a ring at the door. Martin managed to stand first. "I'll get it, Faith." He touched her arm.

"Thank you."

Arthur looked down at his t-shirt and took a big swallow of coffee, wincing as it burned on the way down. "Let me grab a quick shower and I'll come and hold up my end of the hosting."

———

BY THREE Arthur thought he would go nuts if he had to take another bite of sympathetic bundt cake or make any more small talk with the church support committee. The Martin Grove Normal Human act was slowly improving, if becoming no less eerie.

Finally, Jennine came by and Arthur decided it was time to bite the bullet.

"Mom?" He cornered his mother in the kitchen to keep the inevitable fight away from the guests. "Um... I need to step out for a bit." Her face went hard. "Deal with things."

"You're going to see *her.* See *them.*" There was a hiss in her voice that came out at no other time.

"I need to do this."

"No, you don't. They're not-"

"They're my half-sisters." Arthur cut her off. "And I promise when I get back you can yell and scream and use all the four-letter words you want and say all the things you should have shouted at dad but were too good a wife to say."

She folded her arms tight. "He never stopped loving her."

He pulled his mom into a hug. She didn't uncross her arms or relax her posture. "He loved you as well."

"How can you know that?"

"He ate your cooking, didn't he? Every bite."

His mother gave a tiny chuckle in spite of herself. Arthur placed a kiss on the side of her head, grounding himself in the familiar scent of her shampoo and perfume, unchanged since he was born.

"Tomorrow let's pick out a box to put dad in, then break out the demon gin and get really, really mad at him before we have to be polite again."

She nodded and muttered an 'okay' into his shoulder before he finally let her go.

————

THE OLD Saigon restaurant could easily seat sixty people and had a separate banquet room. It was the third and largest location Hanh had owned in Arthur's lifetime and the sixth since that first noodle shop. She said it was as big as she could handle now. It wasn't fancy. There weren't set places with cloth napkins. Instead, the chopsticks sat in large cups in the middle of tables next to the bottles of chili oil and fish sauce.

Not fancy didn't mean unpopular. Even at the strange hour of four in the afternoon, there were still a half dozen people in the dining room. He could feel Martin next to him, a calm steady presence. He wanted to reach out and take Martin's hand, feel that contact, ground himself on the warmth of human touch. Instead he waved off the waitress who approached, he didn't recognize her, and headed straight for the kitchen.

It was about as quiet as a professional kitchen ever gets. There was mostly the sound of chopping, the bubbling of soups and stocks, mixed in with the hiss of the industrial dishwasher. His sisters were there and Hanh but no one else, which was unusual. Hanh approached him, her face stony and still, the lines carved in around her eyes and mouth as if chiseled into granite. Her eyes were still sharp, though, as she looked him over. She hardly came up to his chin, but in his mind, she was large, looming over him, her lips pinched tight. He had been nearly ten before he began to really understand what he was to her. The blue eyed, legitimate son of the man she bore three illegitimate daughters to, placed under her roof every weekend and for two weeks in the summer while his own mother volunteered at a bible camp. She was never particularly kind to him but she was never cruel. She made him work, but that was no different from her own children.

He was well into his teens before he recognized her raw

strength. Leaving her shattered country with a soldier she hardly knew, with little more than the clothes on her back. Dismissed by other refugees for her French blood and family name. Raising three daughters with only sporadic help, and growing a tiny noodle shop into a local institution. And putting up with both him and his father.

"You're here to work," she finally said. It wasn't a question. It wouldn't have been even if he didn't have his roll of knives tucked under his arm.

"Yes."

She cast a cool look over Martin. "Who's he?"

"Martin Grove. He's a friend from work."

"Can he wash dishes?"

"Yes ma'am, I can." There was a tiny quirk to Martin's lips as the two sized each other up. Their faces still and their eyes speaking volumes. They were a pair, but Hanh had more practice.

"Good. Eduardo got deported yesterday."

Arthur would have been surprised if whoever got deported was actually called Eduardo. She used the name in reference to the never-ending stream of undocumented kitchen help who would show up at the back door, cousin, brother, friend of the previous Eduardo, with their own knives and chef's whites, and step neatly into whichever vacant spot there was. There would probably be three more by lunch prep tomorrow, but for that night, it looked like it would be him, his sisters, and Martin. It wasn't the first time they'd done this, though it might possibly be the last.

Hanh pointed Martin to the dishes and Arthur to a ten-pound cold box of shrimp.

He pushed up his sleeves and grabbed an apron before sliding into place next to Sonia, who was filleting fish with a little more aggression than was possibly necessary. "Dad has crap timing," she growled without looking up at him.

"Is that supposed to be news?"

"I've got a soft opening on Friday and I'm fighting with my berry supplier."

"Number three?"

"Four. Dessert bistro."

"Nice." Hanh might have built an established restaurant but Sonia had built a small, if ever growing, restaurant empire she was ruling with an iron fist.

"Hard to do a chocolate cake with raspberry reduction when you're getting screwed on the price of raspberries."

"Cake still sounds nice."

Sonia just grunted and threw a fish skeleton into a stock pot with considerable force. They didn't talk after that. Arthur did his best not to even think beyond what had to be done next. Shrimp, vegetables, sauces, noodles cooked and cooled. The orders started to come in. They shouted at each other, words he seldom spoke anymore flowing effortlessly over his tongue, a garbled mess of French, Vietnamese, English, and bits of Spanish left by various Eduardos. He sprinkled some thin sliced red onion over the top of a plate of Bo Tai Chanh, feeling more at home than he did in his mother's parlor, and yelled for the next order.

He glanced over to Martin a few times. His white shirt was stuck to his still thin body with sweat and the steam from the dishes, but he worked without hesitation or question, never once dropping a dish or getting in someone's way. Occasionally they looked up at the same moment and again Arthur wanted to take his hand, give it a squeeze, and somehow become part of that cool grace.

———

IT WAS closing in on eleven before the last customers cleared out, but without comment there was one more set of orders. Arthur assembled a dozen more rolls and took them out to one of the larger tables. Sonia laid out big bowls of pho while Roselyne brought out plates of vegetables and meat. And for the six of them, Yvette laid out a dozen beers. Arthur was sure he'd be drinking at least four of them.

They sat, still sweaty from the kitchen, hardly speaking, and began to eat and drink, the hunger and exhaustion kicking in. He put a roll on Martin's plate out of old lunch habits and Martin picked up a pair of chopsticks. It had only been a couple of weeks earlier that he had started trying to teach Martin how to use them.

He put them into place one at a time and slowly, with great concentration, he tried to pick up the roll. Everyone else at the table slowed down their own eating to watch. Arthur flushed with embarrassment. If he'd known he would be bringing Martin here, he would have started teaching him months ago. As it was, he'd just have to manage.

It was like watching a video of the space station's robot arm trying to catch a satellite knowing they would only really have one chance.

Not too tight. Just enough to raise it.

Arthur gave a little internal cheer as Martin got it off the plate on the first try. He got it to his mouth, took a bite, then squeezed too hard. It fell back to the plate, half disintegrating on the way.

There were some small chuckles and the mood lightened at the table.

Sonia upended her first beer before letting out a long sigh. "I'm guessing there's no point in me asking, but when's the funeral?"

Arthur took a long drink of his own beer. Thin and a bit bitter, it was still cold enough to go down easily. "Saturday. It'll be at the VA hall so..."

"Faith will not want us there," Hanh snapped. It was the first thing Hanh had said to him in hours.

"She doesn't get a choice." Arthur snapped back.

"Are you going to tell her that?" Yvette asked with a sneer in her voice. The youngest of the three, they had never fully gotten along.

"Yes." Arthur finished his beer in one very long pull. "And it will be a fucking mess and I will deal with it."

"Don't swear at the table."

He pulled the top off another beer. He'd managed to forget for a moment. With half-cramped hands, sore feet, and the taste of cheap imported beer, he'd convinced himself he was sixteen again for a moment and it was a Sunday night and after they ate his dad would drive them home so they would be there when his mother returned on Monday morning.

"Dad was..." he didn't even know how to finish that sentence. "Mom would never divorce him, you would never marry him, and his idea of responsibility was to try to have his cake and eat it too. This is what we have now, so on Saturday at—"

"Ten thirty," Martin provided.

"Ten thirty, everyone can front up at the VA hall. Listen to someone give a eulogy."

"Your mother wants you to do it."

Fuck my life.

"Sure. Fine. Listen to *me* mumble something about dad that doesn't make him sound like a total jerk, then we all take a deep breath and just... We just take a deep breath."

"Fuck that fucking bastard," Roselyne muttered and didn't react to her mother hitting her on the arm for language.

Martin dropped his roll again. Hanh looked him over. "You don't eat enough."

It was Arthur's turn to try to hold back the laughter.

Martin sighed. "So I've been told."

————

MARTIN WAS warm. Arthur tried not to lean too heavily on him as he stumbled through the restaurant doors, but he'd had too many beers and it was well after midnight. Martin steered him to the passenger's side of the car. He could have probably made it himself with a bit of work but there was something nice about Martin manhandling him and he let it happen.

Things had relaxed a bit. They drank and cursed his father's name and watched Martin get through two rolls and some noodles while holding the chopsticks in a death grip of stubbornness. He didn't tell his sisters it was more than he'd ever seen him eat ever for any reason. He leaned his cheek on the side of Martin's head.

"'M proud you," he mumbled as Martin shoved him into the passenger's seat.

"Thank you." He couldn't tell if Martin was amused or just bored with his behavior. It would be easier to tell if he could see him but his eyes were feeling a bit unfocused. It was hard enough to catch those little quirks and twitches when sober.

"'M gonna teach you to cook," Arthur stated with the certainty of a drunk. "Not hard and you're smart."

"Buckle yourself in."

He fumbled with the straps, yanking them several times before managing to pull them across his body and click them in place. The seat seemed deeper than he remembered and he felt as though he was sinking through it, maybe right down to the ground under them. He kept his eyes on Martin as he slid into the driver's seat of his father's car, his face as still as if they were at work. It wasn't right.

"I like seeing you smile on Saturdays. You're so... Those kids love you. You should be a teacher not-," he waved an arm around trying to convey the whole grand idea of the Agency. "They make you happy. You should be happy. You're not happy at work, I can tell."

"Neither are you."

Arthur tried to form an argument, but even sober he didn't think he'd be able to. "You're good with the kids. You just get them or something."

"Children are simple. They want support, the opportunity to learn, safety to fail, and when they lash out, it is in fear or frustration. Easy enough to manage."

"But not grownups. Grownups suck. That's why you don't smile at grownups."

"A child who is disappointed can be difficult. An adult who is disappointed is dangerous."

Arthur closed his eyes. He felt sad and heavy and the dark seemed warm. "'m not dangerous." He blindly reached out and tried to land a hand on Martin's shoulder.

Martin sighed. "Everyone is dangerous."

CHAPTER TEN

THIS TIME, Arthur did have a proper hangover as he fumbled to turn off the alarm on his phone. His whole body ached. He could feel the pounding of his pulse in his head, hands, and feet. His mouth was dry and rancid and his skin sticky with dried sweat. He slowly took a breath through his nose, trying to keep the contents of his stomach down. He could smell the shrimp cooked into his skin.

He wanted to roll over, sink back into sleep, but he knew he needed to get up. He had to help pick out a coffin. His mother needed to yell at him and he had a feeling he needed to apologize to Martin. He thinks he might have tried to touch Martin's lips the night before but he honestly couldn't remember if he tried it or just thought about trying it. He does know he spent most of the drive home just staring at his profile highlighted in small bursts as they slid past street lamps.

He rolled from bed and shuffled to the bathroom. It was too difficult to think clearly so he got himself clean and ready for the day on autopilot while letting his mind just jump around and settle where it wanted to. It mostly seemed to jump between snips of conversations with Martin and, for some reason, number stations, though he wasn't sure how they might be related.

He smiled and tried to look fine when he joined his mother and

Martin at the breakfast table, but his hand shook badly as he reached for some orange juice. "Hi." His voice was rough.

His mother didn't look at him, instead remained focused on the six-sheet community newspaper. "We're going to look at coffins and flowers in fifteen minutes, then choose a plot. Something I asked your father to do five years ago, but he refused."

He glanced to Martin who was back to the Mister Rogers look. He was focused on something on his laptop.

"Sure. Let me just..." He held up his orange juice then chugged it, hoping desperately it would stay down, his stomach now churning as much from guilt as anything else.

———

LOOKING AT coffins was surreal. That one of his few friends from high school was selling them just made it extra weird. He'd owned cars with fewer features than some of the caskets. He knew his dad would have been happy with just a plain wood box, but it wasn't that easy. Martin was yet again a saving grace, helping to steer his mother towards plainer but tasteful options and distract her while Arthur talked to his friend about cost.

The florist was much the same and, for as much as he tried to focus on casket toppers and graveside displays, he kept watching Martin.

Everyone is dangerous.

And Martin seemed to dance around that danger, coming across as smiling, charming, sweet, harmless, no threat. It was graceful, beautiful, and horrible. Shell and illusions, carefully constructed feelings and personality layered over and over.

It was only when he was standing on a piece of neatly trimmed grass, a man in a dark suit commenting on the lovely view of nothing interesting did he catch a quick glimpse through the layers. There was a slow gust of wind, unseasonably warm. Martin turned his face towards it, his hair ruffling, his eyes closed, and his lips parted. The sun fell on his face in a way that made him look younger, or perhaps made him look his age. Arthur still wasn't sure.

He did know he wanted to step close to Martin, to wrap his

arms around him, hold him tight, thank him for everything and apologize for whatever dangers in his past he had known.

The wind died away and a cloud settled over the sun.

"I think your father would have liked this place." There was a crack in his mother's voice.

He would not have given a shit.

"Yeah. I think it's a good spot."

CHAPTER ELEVEN

THE NEXT few days blurred together: smiling politely for visitors he didn't know, soothing his mother, sorting through his father's things. At least the bastard had been smart enough to leave a will, but there were still clothes, books, and bits and pieces his mother didn't want. They didn't get around to the fight they should have had.

And through all of it there was Martin, calm and cool, picking up every dropped ball, and remembering every detail. Sometimes dressed like Mr. Rogers, other times like a secret agent, he felt like the only real thing in hazed-out chaos.

On the morning of the funeral, Arthur found his black suit perfectly pressed, and his shoes shined and waiting for him when he woke. There was also a blank pad and a pen, a subtle reminder that he might want to actually write his father's eulogy.

He'd been avoiding that. Every time he sat down to try, all that came out was a string of expletives and insults.

In the living room, he found his mother dressed in dark blue. "I just couldn't wear black," she said even before good morning. "I look just awful in black and that's such a vain thing to say. Your father never liked me in black and-"

He gently pulled her close, careful not to wrinkle her dress. "You look fine. It's okay." He felt a tremor run through her and she pulled away.

"Nope." Her voice was tight. "No tears yet."

Martin appeared from somewhere holding out a box of tissue. "Thank you, dear."

He glanced at Martin. He was actually wearing a black suit. Properly black instead of the very dark gray of his work clothes. And not just the suit, but his shirt and tie were black as well.

Arthur looked away because it hadn't been real before that. Picking a coffin, sorting his clothes, trying to write a eulogy, none of it had been real until he saw Martin dressed in black. It was like a brick slammed into his chest and he clenched his jaw tight. His father was dead. In a few minutes, he would drive to the VA Hall, attend his father's funeral, then bury him under some grass with a view of nothing interesting. It was happening. It was real. His father was gone and it hurt.

A hand was rested on his shoulder. It was nearly as fine and light as his mother's but it seemed to ground him into the Earth like the roots of a tree.

"We should go."

"Yeah," Arthur nodded resisting the urge to take Martin's hand and pull him close. "We don't want to be late.

———

ARTHUR LOOKED over the crowd. More people had shown up than he expected. He recognized most of them. There were guys from his dad's old unit that he would meet up with every so often. Guys from the lumber yard where he used to work. Guys he hung out with at the bar. On one side was his mother and her friends from church, there for support. On the other was Hanh and his sisters. It was Martin's fast feet and quick words that had kept the two groups apart.

Some minister he didn't recognize had spoken. One of his dad's old war buddies told a story he'd heard a thousand times but instantly forgot. Then he was gestured to stand. He looked down at the piece of paper clutched in his hand; his final failed attempt at writing a eulogy in advance.

He looked back up, his heart beginning to race and his mouth going dry. His eyes skimmed over the crowd, desperate for a life-line of some sort. His gaze fell on Martin, sitting in the back, calm and still like a stone that had to be built around, impossible to move.

"My father contradicted himself." The borrowed words came without conscience thought. "He contained multitudes." Arthur felt his heart begin to settle. "There are many in this room today who loved Jason Drams. And there are many who hated him. And for the most part they are the same people. This is the eulogy I tried to write." He held up the crumpled paper. "It's just the word 'bastard' written about fifty times. And he would have been the first to agree with that assessment. He would probably have wanted me to read it word for word, laughing the whole time. He was contradictions. He loved this place, but railed against its small-town mindset. He was proud to have served and horrified by things he did while serving. He could work himself half to death yet still seem lazy. Give you the shirt off his back, but still seem cheap. He loved so many people so deeply, but could never quite work out how not to hurt them. He judged no one, when he was judged by so many." There was a crack in his voice and a burn in his throat. He locked his eyes on Martin, a solid lifeline. "And he inspired love and devotion in those who should have probably just walked away. He tried to be a good man, at the end of the day. He was a good man. He had his faults, flaws, and there were things he just screwed up royally, but he acknowledged those. He never tried to present himself as something other than what he was. A loving, charming, big hearted, total bastard." He quickly wiped away a tear that had escaped. "There are grumpy, half-frozen crows on the lawn outside. They don't know that a man who was loved has died and even if they did, they wouldn't care. He'd tell us not to be maudlin, not to cry. He'd want a party in his name and be disappointed if at least one person didn't pass out. He was a good man, and for all his flaws, that's how I will try to remember him."

Arthur sat back down, his pulse pounding in his ears. His mother took his hands and leaned against his shoulder. The minister got back up, said something Arthur didn't really hear. His mother gave him a push when it was time to lift the casket. It seemed so short. He was sure his father had been taller. Some of his dad's old army buddies, the ones in better health, helped him make the slow procession to the hearse. People started to mill around. Only a few would head up to the burial, the rest would avoid the biting wind. Jennine said she'd go back to the house to set up the little luncheon.

He spotted Hanh and his sisters at the edge of the crowd, watching. A flash of rage, for a moment, overwhelmed the grief. It wasn't right. Hanh loved his father. She should be the one rallied around and cared for as the grieving widow, instead of being seen as some foreign mistress, their love somehow worthless, despite all their years. Martin followed his gaze, then stepped up to his mother, handing her tissues and turning her away, speaking softly as she did.

Arthur pushed past the guests, each wanting a moment to express sympathy and stopped in front of Hanh. Her eyes were red but there was no sign of shed tears. He pulled her close and he felt her arms go up around him holding him tight, strong from years of hard work.

"I'm sorry," he said softly, trying to apologize for himself, his father, society and every other drop of bullshit he could think of. She nodded against his chest then pulled away. He hugged each of his sisters, next muttering some words they all knew were useless, but they were the kind of things you said anyway. He hugged Sonia last.

"Are you going to come back?" she asked.

"Can I get a reservation at your dessert place?"

"No, but if you get fired I'll let you wash dishes."

They both smiled as much as they could. "Thanks." He hugged her again.

"You know you've got more balls than I ever thought, bringing your boyfriend to this."

"He's not my—"

"Whatever." She gave him one more quick hug. "Don't be a stranger."

"You, too."

———

IT WAS only standing at the grave site that the little niggling thought that he was forgetting something sprang fully formed. He wanted to lean over and whisper to Martin, a thread of almost panic in him, but he had placed himself at the back of the small crowd. The minister recited prayers and Arthur held his mother as she finally, properly cried. He wasn't ready yet.

When they began to shuffle over the dried winter grass to the cars, he managed to slide back to Martin.

"Who's at the library today?"

"I left instructions for Julia to present the lessons today. She is nearly twelve and showing leadership capabilities."

"Good. Okay. It just hit me and I couldn't believe I forgot."

Martin smiled a little. "You've had other things on your mind."

———

THE HOUSE was already filled when they arrived home from the cemetery. They separated him from his mother quickly, the ladies setting her down on the couch and handing her cake while men who had known his father patted him on the back and told stories about him that he'd already heard but was willing to hear one more time. Martin slid through the crowd in his black suit, giving off the feeling that he was stage managing the whole thing, maximum expressions of condolences with minimal drama.

It was, however, Jennine who took a small flask from a pocket and poured a helping into his coffee.

"Thank you."

"You looked like you were going to shove a cake fork into your head if you had to listen to one more war story sober."

He took a sip of his coffee, now sweet with rum. "I needed this. Don't suppose you could slip some of that to my mom?" he joked.

"Already did."

"Does she know that?!" As far as he knew, his mother had never taken a drink in her life.

Jennine smiled at him. "Your mother can drink and smoke and

knows every four-letter word in the book. She just always insisted on being proper in front of you to make up for..." She waved a hand, somehow summing up his entire life and his parents' relationship in a simple gesture.

He tried to picture his mother cussing. He couldn't. "She didn't have to."

"No, she didn't. But she did. Lot of things she didn't have to, but she did."

———

IT WAS evening by the time the last of the guests left and Arthur was drunk. He sat down on the couch next to his mother. Her cheeks were flushed and she was blinking slowly.

"You're drunk." He was too far gone to filter his words.

"So are you." She leaned against his side. "I liked what you said about your father." Her words came soft and slow and her breath smelled of coffee and rum.

"Even though I cussed?"

"He was a fucking bastard of a bastard bastard."

Arthur choked then began to laugh. The laughter shook his body and he couldn't stop, couldn't begin to rein it in. Somewhere though, the laughter turned to tears he had no more hope of stopping. He wrapped his arms around his mother and felt her hiccupping sobs against his chest. They stayed like that for a long time, the sobs becoming giggles becoming sobs again. Finally, when they pulled apart, they found fresh glasses of water and a box of tissues waiting for them.

CHAPTER TWELVE

ON TUESDAY, Arthur stumbled back into the office after a late-night flight; the budget airline feeling that much more terrifying in the dark.

Martin had gotten the flight with him and managed to sleep the whole way while Arthur had a death grip on his arm rests. When the turbulence did manage to settle out, he'd take a few minutes to watch Martin sleep. His hands were folded neatly in his lap and his head tilted back. He couldn't help thinking how vulnerable it made him look, throat exposed to the world, and Arthur resisted the urge to tilt his head down. His face was animated in sleep, more so than when he was awake. His lips moved as if he were whispering to someone. There would be flashes of smiles or frowns. He wanted to lean in close to see if he could catch those whispered words and discover some secret key to Martin's mind. That half remembered drunken urge to touch those lips returned.

He was half asleep himself when he pinned the sheet for the Super Bowl pool in the break room. Turns out it just involved printing out a grid and writing numbers on it later. Carol tapped him on the shoulder.

"Hey, you're back. I heard about your dad. How are you holding up?"

Arthur shrugged and didn't ask how she knew. "We haven't

exactly been close since I left home but, I don't know, still feels weird."

"At least you had your boyfriend for support."

"He's not my boyfriend."

Carol smiled and patted him on the arm. "Yes, he is and I think you know it."

Arthur was going to argue more but the guy who sat a few cubes down, Andrew maybe, came in.

"Hey, Super Bowl pool! Who's running it?" he asked Arthur and Carol.

"I am. Five bucks a square." Arthur replied despite the fact that his name and cubicle coordinates were on the bottom of the sheet.

"Cool. I don't have cash today but I'll swing by your desk tomorrow."

"No problem."

———

ARTHUR HADN'T been able to put himself together much of a lunch. He hadn't cleaned his fridge before he left and had returned home to find mostly wilted vegetables and meat past its best-by date. Best he'd been able to manage was some boiled eggs, good cheese, a bit of salami, and some cherry tomatoes that had held up over the week, and at lunch they slipped right back into routine. Martin had his alien face back on and was reading *The Food of a Younger Land: The WPA's Portrait of Food in Pre-World War II America*. Arthur had found his copy of Tolkien's Beowulf in his desk drawer where he left it, and they sat reading in silence with Arthur pushing food in Martin's direction. Arthur luxuriated in the moment. After a week of chaos and swinging emotions, to sit there quiet, across from Martin, reading a book, was like slipping into a warm bath.

Someone tapped him on the shoulder. He turned to see one of the guys who always gave him weird looks smiling and holding a five-dollar bill.

I'm going to kill someone.

BY SATURDAY, most of the guys who had given him weird looks his first week on the floor had filled their names on the paper grid and were giving him less weird looks. Several gave condolences as they did. Arthur still didn't ask how that had gotten around. They were gossipy secret agents.

The children at the library were happy to have Merlin and Arthur back, but reported that Julia had done a good job filling in. Merlin smiled at them, collected neatly penned homework, and began the Odyssey, though in English instead of ancient Greek. Apparently, there were even limits to his knowledge of obscure languages. He still managed to find a rhythm though and Arthur could picture him in a Greek court, reciting by torch light to the notes of a lyre. He smiled and the children were enraptured.

"I WAS wondering if you'd like to come back to my place this afternoon?" Arthur asked as Martin picked up next week's books, his stomach doing flips, worried that he might just be about to ruin the most enjoyable part of his life. Martin froze, his face going blank. "I said I'd teach you to cook," he added quickly, not wanting Martin to get the wrong impression. He'd remembered that much from his night of serious drinking. "It's really a pretty analytical endeavor at the start."

Martin said nothing and Arthur stayed silent not wanting to sound pushy or dig himself a hole.

"Yes," Martin finally replied. Behind Martin the reference librarian gave Arthur a big grin and double thumbs up.

ARTHUR HAD spent days contemplating exactly what he should do for Martin's first lesson. He tried to remember what, of all the things he'd fed Martin, he'd responded to the best. Eggs were usually a good place to start when teaching someone how to cook, but they could also be a bit plain. What he wanted was something easy, but not too easy, Martin was no idiot.

"Croque Monsieur. Ever had it?"

"No." Martin had removed his coat and rolled up his sleeves, but there was a stiffness to him again that Arthur had not seen for a while.

"It's a French style ham and grilled cheese sandwich that literally translates into Mister Crunch. It's a little more complicated than something you make in a dorm room and so much better. Ideally you use Gruyere cheese and a Béchamel sauce, which is really easy to make and everyone should know how." Arthur pulled the ingredients from his fridge as he talked, not wanting to seem like he was lecturing. He'd gone for best quality everything and it was likely to be the most expensive grilled cheese sandwich in history, but if there was one thing in his life he wasn't going to half-ass, it was this.

He handed Martin a small pot and a whisk then took out a pot and whisk for himself. "We'll start with the Béchamel sauce. The trick is not to let it get too hot and to keep the right proportion of butter, flour, and milk. And really, every sauce you will ever make is about keeping the right proportion of fat, starch, and liquid. If you can manage this, the rest is just riffing on a theme."

Arthur had to throw out his after it burned. He was too busy being distracted by Martin's, which came out perfectly on the first try. Martin smiled.

CHAPTER THIRTEEN

LIFE AT the Agency was very much about routine. Arriving, finding analysis assignments in the inbox then reading, translating, writing briefings and suggestions that everyone believed were never actually read. Sometimes some part of the world would go a bit nuts, or come close to it, and the few people with the right background would work like mad for a few days, then it would all settle back down again. It was boring, but the pay was decent, the benefits good, and his level of analysis was unlikely to ever be hit by resource reallocation or administrative changes.

Outside of the rules of the Agency, Arthur had found another routine. Quiet lunches. Books read in silence, yet with a sense of togetherness. Saturdays at the library, then going back to his place for cooking lessons. Sometimes the lessons would run late and turn into dinner at retro movie theaters. It was a comfortable routine, but a happy one, and as winter crawled towards spring, Martin was prone to smiling more easily, and eating a bit more. When Arthur dropped a whisk, flipping whipped cream across himself, Martin laughed a proper laugh. Sometimes their hands would brush over ingredients or books and Arthur felt warm and a little happier.

———

ROUTINES BREAK. That is their nature.

Martin had a precision routine for his tea, so when Arthur heard the swivel of a chair and footsteps behind him at the wrong time, he looked over his shoulder

Martin was standing there so still it seemed unnatural. A phone was clutched in his hand. His eyes locked onto Arthur's. Arthur said nothing. Whatever was going on, the words that needed to be said were not his. Finally, he raised his hand and touched his fingers to his forehead. "I can give you this." He lowered his hand and pressed the tips of his fingers to the center of his chest. "And I can give you this. But not the rest. It's not who I am. Or what I am."

Arthur nodded unsure what to say or even to think. Martin gave a small nod in return before turning into the depths of the cubicle labyrinth. Arthur didn't turn back to his computer, instead he stared at the gray gap where Martin had been.

Head and heart but not the rest. Not his body? His job? His past? Did he even want those things? Did Martin want anything in return?

He knew Martin had his head. His peace, and intelligence, and very dry humor had slid into his own mind. His days didn't feel right without it. His heart? Carol referred to Martin as his boyfriend and refused any arguments to the contrary. And he was listed as such on some hospital documents. Arthur had never had a boyfriend, or girlfriend. He'd had dates sometimes with the same person more than once, but they never lasted long enough to apply terms. The rush for sex in his younger years had been off-putting in ways he knew didn't line up with others his age. And the lies to dates when he was older were equally off-putting.

Outside of an occasional desire to weave their fingers together and trying to eyeball his weight, he'd never considered access to Martin's body.

A child who is disappointed can be difficult. An adult who is disappointed is dangerous.

Were there others who had been disappointed? Others who became dangers, wanting more than what Martin was willing or able to give?

Arthur closed his eyes and took deep long breaths. He felt sick and a little dizzy.

Head and heart. He'd take them if offered and he'd give them in return. He already had.

We'll have to talk.

———

ARTHUR LOOKED first to the table he usually shared with Martin. He wasn't surprised that it was empty as Martin had yet to return to his cubicle, but there was a little disappointment. He sat down with Carol instead.

"Boyfriend not in town, so I get the honor of your company."

He pushed across the table a small Tupperware box. "Home-made baklava."

"You are forgiven."

In teaching Martin to cook, he'd been trying to expand his own day-to-day repertoire, but the baklava had still taken a half dozen attempts to get right. Phyllo dough was not forgiving. He opened his own lunch of a Caesar salad, but didn't feel hungry. He picked the croutons out and crunched on those.

"So, what happened?"

Arthur looked up. "What?"

"That's more than 'my boyfriend ditched out on lunch' glum."

"I'm fine." The bog standard social nicety fell from his lips.

"No, you're not. Did you fight?"

"No," he snapped.

"Nah, he doesn't seem the fighting type. Make you vanish type maybe."

Arthur just grumbled and picked at his salad. He was aware of Carol's scrutiny.

"Okay."

Arthur looked up and saw her grin.

"I'm going to take a guess. Did someone screw up the 'I love you' moment?" He wasn't sure what look must have crossed his face before he got it under control, but Carol winced. "Oh, you did."

"No. It wasn't—"

Yes, it was, you idiot.

"I just mean...." Arthur pressed his face into his hand. He'd screwed up the 'I love you' moment.

"Yeah." Carol dragged out the word. "That one's going to hurt for a while."

"He didn't actually say it." Arthur tried to defend himself.

"But he did, didn't he?"

He wanted to bang his head on the table, but it would only fuel rumors.

"Do you want advice?"

"No."

"Do you love him?"

"Yes."

"Have you told him?"

"No."

"Go tell him. That's the advice you didn't want."

Arthur picked up some croutons and crunched them far harder than he needed to. "Why am I your friend?" he asked.

"Because you eat lunch with the weird kid in class. And every pretty gay boy needs a tough, hardcore lesbian in their corner and every tough lesbian needs a pretty gay boy for balance. It's in the rule book."

"I'm not that pretty."

"And I'm not that hardcore, but we make do."

Arthur tried to disconnect and just let random thoughts bounce around his head. "I'm not that gay either."

"Okay, pretty little bi boys."

He frowned. That didn't feel right. It never had, but he never put a lot of thought into what did. "I don't think that's right either."

"Well, you aren't straight."

Arthur felt a headache coming on. "I don't know. None of it ever—" He tried to convey his meaning by stabbing his salad.

"You know there are more options these days? Asexual, demi-sexual, graysexual, omnisexual, bisexual, pansexual. It's like Bron-tosauruses."

"What?" Arthur was sure he couldn't have heard that right.

"You know, when we were kids there was like T-rex, Tricer-atops, and Brontosaurs. Now there's Brachiosaurus, Diplodocus,

Qijianglong, Dreadnoughtus. They find a new one every six months."

Arthur stared at her, suddenly considering his sexuality in terms of long necked dinosaurs. Carol sighed.

"My girlfriend's a paleontologist. Would you like to know why every dinosaur toy on the market is completely wrong?"

"If you think it will distract me from my own brain while I finish this salad, sure."

———

MARTIN HADN'T returned to his cubicle by the end of the day and his parking spot was empty. Arthur had never had an assignment that took him out of the building, but then he was pretty damn sure Martin was not a level 2 analyst and was maybe something closer to an actual secret agent. He drove six blocks from the building and pulled over. He kept Martin's number in his head instead of his phone. Old School. It went to messages after a half dozen rings. Wherever it was, it was turned on.

"Hey, it's me. I thought about what you said and I understand. At least I think I understand. I'm pretty sure I understand and I'm okay. Really." He took a big breath. "Nothing more than you're willing to give. I'm not dangerous. I promise. Call me back okay."

Arthur closed his eyes and waited, hoping Martin would call right back, but there was nothing.

The next day Martin's parking spot and cubicle were still empty.

The safety of the country could hinge on a tiny detail you pick up. Arthur recited the motto of one of his prime training lectures as he tried to focus on his work: drug cartels trying to destabilize a government. Could be an opportunity to let it happen, then swoop in and get someone willing to play ball in power, but a risky move. He left out that last bit of his analysis. It wasn't his job to suggest black ops foreign policy. It was an easy observation and someone higher up would undoubtedly make it. He heard footsteps coming down the hall and looked over his shoulder, but it was just one of the other analysts walking by.

THERE WERE six rings and a voice told him to leave a message.

"Hey, me again. I'm going to drop by your place. Make sure you didn't slip in the shower or something. You know me. I worry. Anyway, if you're not there, I'll leave. I mean if you're not there, you're not going to know anyway but I'm trying not to be a creep. Bye."

HE KNOCKED on Martin's door for a solid minute before letting himself in. His car hadn't been in the building's lot but his key still slipped neatly in.

"Hello?"

There was no response. It took less than five minutes to search the place. His heart pounded the whole time waiting to find Martin sprawled on the floor. He wasn't sure if he felt better or worse to find the place empty. His painting was still on the wall and his fine china tea dishes in the cupboard. He pressed his hands over his face.

"Get your shit together," he muttered aloud. "We are—"

Arthur went silent.

We are secret agents.

There had been some field agent style training even for the desk jockey analysts. It was mostly how to tell if you're being followed, checking for bugs in your own home, and spotting honey traps. He started to search the apartment again, looking for much smaller items. He used the screwdriver on his pocket knife to check behind plugs and switch plates. He tapped light bulbs, flipped through the pages of the library books, checked under drawers and in closets. He found a cardboard box in a closet filled with identical suits and Mr. Rogers' sweaters. Inside were files with the names of all the library students. They were filled with hand-written homework as well as personal notes by Martin noting progress and development.

There were no bugs Arthur could find.

CHAPTER FOURTEEN

ARTHUR HAD never considered himself the anxious type, but by Saturday he was twitching. Carol had tried to calm him and keep his mind off it and he now knew more about dinosaurs than he could have imagined, but there was still that nagging unease and the urge to turn around every time he heard footsteps in the hall.

When he put a stack of library books on the reference desk, he hoped to hear that Martin was already in the children's section waiting, but there was no luck there.

The children looked up at him. "Merlin is on a... I guess you can call it a business trip. So, I'll be filling in." He smiled trying to put out an aura of calm and confidence.

"When will he be back?" one of the younger children asked.

"Not entirely sure, but probably not long." The children all frowned at him. "Don't worry. This time I know what I'm doing and," he picked up the copy of the *Iliad* they'd been working on. "We're reading a modern English translation." The children all gave him the hard eye. He wasn't their Merlin but he would have to do for now.

———

HE LISTENED to the six rings and the voice telling him to leave a message while he unpacked his groceries.

"Hi. So, I didn't butcher the *Iliad* as badly as *Beowulf*. Dropped off your books. Brought in your mail, it was starting to build up. Jung was the quote of the week. 'Your visions will become clear only when you can look into your own heart. Who looks outside, dreams; who looks inside, awakes.' I don't know. Seems appropriate. Been looking inside myself a lot lately for what it's worth. Anyways, look I know it's more than just you and me listening to this. I don't even know if you're getting these messages, but Andrew, if you're the one listening to this, you owe me twenty bucks from the Super Bowl pool. Stop being a cheap bastard. And if it's not Andrew, tell him he owes me twenty bucks and to stop being a cheap bastard."

———

"HE'S STILL not back." Carol sounded sympathetic. She'd stopped teasing him about missing his boyfriend after the first week he was gone. Arthur slowly stirred the milk into his coffee.

"His phone started going direct to voice mail." He was waiting for, and dreading the day, he called to leave a message and only got three tones and a voice telling him the number had been disconnected and was no longer in service.

"I'm sorry."

He shrugged. There was literally not a single thing he could do except to read to the children on Saturdays and bring in the mail and leave steadily longer and more rambling messages. He took a sip of coffee, not really tasting it. "I think I'm demisexual. Maybe. It would explain some things, but I'm not sure. It's all just, I don't know. Maybe I've been thinking too much."

She patted his arm. "Perfectly valid. And no one ever said you have to define yourself. I mean, some people feel better with a definitive definition, others don't. You're you, first and foremost, and don't let anyone tell you otherwise."

"Thanks. This is why pretty boys need their hard-core lesbians."

Carol grinned at him. "You're not that pretty."

"And you're not that hard core."

———

THE STACK of mail he dropped on Martin's table was thick, heavy, and full of envelopes bearing the seals of private academies. He hadn't opened any of the mail so far. There were none that said 'Over Due Last Warning' so he figured the bills must be on some automatic payment. But he decided he was going to open these even if it was a federal offence.

They were information and application packets for some of the best schools in the country. A dozen of them. Private boarding schools that cost more a term than he had paid in college. He put his hands in his face and wanted to cry. "Come home, come home."

He dialed a number.

"Hey. Brought in your mail. Whole bunch of school information packets. Exeter. Seriously, even I've heard of fucking Exeter. I get it. I get what you're trying to do. Those kids deserve so much better than the shit-hole public schools they're in. They've got to be going nuts with boredom compared to what you give them. I pity their regular teachers. The thing is, I don't know how to do this. I'm sure you have some plan to get them all the very best. You're good at planning things but I don't know what the plan is. I can only guess you never intended to be away this long or you would have left instructions or a note or something."

Arthur heard his voice crack. He took long deep breaths.

"Anyway, I've started on Jules Verne in the French because, guess what, I can read French and I've read all of Jules Verne. Maybe talk about how science fiction has influenced actual science and technology over the years. And after that, maybe take a step away from the classics for a bit. Girlfriend of a friend is a paleontologist. All kids like dinosaurs even though it turns out most of them were probably a bit fluffy. I keep on picturing a T-rex covered in yellow baby chick fluff. Makes me laugh. You need to come back because your handwriting is way neater than mine and there are a lot of applications to fill out."

———

FOR AN agency that dealt in secrets, people were bad at keeping them. There was a twenty-dollar bill on his desk when he got into work. He stared at it, his gut dropping and his hands beginning to shake. People knew. Or at least people would make assumptions based on his phone messages. He didn't care so much about what they thought of him, but Martin was a man of privacy and secrets. When he came back, and he had to believe there was a when, he would not like the gossip.

All heads swiveled towards him at lunch, then quickly turned back, but not fast enough to miss the looks of sympathy and pity.

He marched to his seat across from Carol head held high.

"People talk," she said kindly.

"Yeah."

"People don't know shit about shit."

Arthur didn't answer. Martin probably spent about 100 bucks a month. Most people had pay go in and bills go out of automatic accounts these days. Depending on how much was sitting in whatever account it could be months, even years, before he got that disconnect message on the phone. A sad dark part of his mind had started to whisper to him that he could be leaving messages for a ghost. "It's been two months," he finally said softly.

"Yeah. I asked Jennifer and she said she'd love to talk to a bunch of kids about dinosaurs."

He gave as much of a smile as he was able. "Thanks. I'm going to introduce her as Guinevere though."

"Why?"

"It's just sort of a thing."

———

IT WAS 3 a.m. and Arthur had been staring at the ceiling for far too long. He picked up his phone. There was one ring, then a computer voice telling him to leave a message.

"Hey, everyone who I know is listening to this, fuck off for like five minutes, seriously five fucking minutes of privacy. Okay?"

Arthur was silent for a few seconds, not really believing this wouldn't be listened to if someone wasn't already listening in live, but it was worth a try.

"It's been three months. Three months since I've seen you or heard from you or anything. I think so much about those last words you said to me. And I didn't say a thing. Just nodded. I understood. I understand. I'm starting to believe you're not coming back. Can't or won't. I don't know which is worse, the idea that you are fine but don't want anything to do with me or the life you had or that something or someone is preventing you from coming back. The second one is worse. The first is just self-pity. I'm afraid I'm leaving messages for a ghost. I'm afraid. It's three in the morning and I'm afraid. I'm going to fill out those forms, all of them for all the kids. No way I can pay for even a fraction. I'll have to ask for financial assistance. And I mean trying to enroll an eight-year-old in Exeter is maybe a little ambitious, but I mean there are parents who get their kids on preschool waiting lists before they're even born so why not. I'm going to keep going. I have to keep going. I know people are still listening to this and someone, some-where must know where you are, or what happened. If someone would please just tell me. Please. It's the not knowing that's really making it hurt."

IT WAS a week later when he found an inter-office envelope on his desk. They were seldom used anymore since they were a giant secu-rity risk. He opened it up. There was a single piece of paper with three words that looked to be actually typed:

We don't know.

Arthur threw-up in the men's room and took the rest of the day off sick.

CHAPTER FIFTEEN

THE LAST time Arthur's phone had rung, it was to be informed of his father's death. It was after two in the morning as Arthur yanked it from its charger on the bedside table.

"Hello," he kept his eyes squeezed shut, the light from the screen blinding.

"Is this Arthur Drams?"

"Yes."

"I'm Doctor Keith calling from Central Hospital, you're listed as the contact for Martin Grove."

Arthur shot up in bed. "He's there? He's alive? Please tell me he's alive, please don't let it be one of these calls, please—"

"He's alive," Dr. Keith cut off his panicked ramble. "He is, however, severely injured and is trying to check himself out. Get down to the emergency room and talk him out of it."

———

THE DRIVE to Central Hospital was forty minutes, except at two in the morning while running red lights and speeding. Then it could be done in fifteen.

He sprinted into the emergency room. "I'm looking for Martin Grove? Is he still here? I got a call."

"Let me check." The nurse at the desk did not seem to be in a huge rush. She probably saw panicked friends and relatives every night of the week. She put down the phone after about thirty seconds of conversation, which felt like an hour to Arthur. "You can go in."

Arthur sprinted through the double doors, only to be stopped by a doctor.

"Agent Drams."

It took Arthur a second to recognize the doctor as the same one from Martin's flu scare. He didn't look any less annoyed than their last meeting. "You called me?"

"Yes. When is the last time you saw Agent Grove?"

"It's been almost four months. Where is he? Is he okay?"

"No." The doctor snapped. "He has what I'm sure is a broken arm, probably broken ribs and toes. He has lacerations that need stitches and infected lacerations that are being held together with what I think is dental floss. All the capillaries in one eye are completely blown, which is a sign of about fifty different things, none of them good. He's gone from skinny to emaciated. And normally when people are chucked out of cars with tinted windows into our ambulance bay, they are kids who've been stabbed in drug deals, not professional adults wearing suits and carrying their keys, phone, and wallet with a government agency ID card. Now he needs medical attention, lots of it, and if you give even a tiny shit about him, you are going to walk into his room and make him stay." There was a hard hiss in the doctor's voice and he looked about ready to hit someone himself.

"Okay," was all Arthur could think to say. The doctor pointed him to some closed curtains at the end of the row.

Where before he had been sprinting, now he stepped with slow trepidation, unsure what he might truly find. He pulled the curtain back slowly. Martin turned his head slightly and looked at him. Half his face was green and yellow with old bruises. The white of his left eye was a deep pink, and from where he was standing, he could see the heavy black bruises and swelling in his right wrist. Arthur had spent months rehearsing all the things he wanted to say but now he had no words.

"I got your messages." Martin's voice was weak and rough.

A sob broke from Arthur's chest. He knelt at the bedside and took Martin's left hand into his. It was thin like an old man's. "I was so worried."

"I'm fine." Martin smiled just a little.

"You are so far from fine it is not even funny and I am not... You are going to stay here. I won't leave your side, not for a second, I promise, but I need you to stay here. I need you to let the doctors take care of you. Please." Arthur didn't try to keep the begging from his voice or the tears from his eyes. "Please."

Martin closed his eyes. "Okay."

"Thank you."

Martin smiled again and his whole body seemed to relax.

The curtain was pulled open and Dr. Keith stepped in. He looked to Arthur. Arthur nodded.

"Okay, let's deal with all the bits that need to be stitched up then I'm going to stick you in a full MRI because god only knows what all is broken or bleeding inside." He looked back to Arthur. "You might want to wait outside for this bit."

"No. I have to stay."

"Fine, whatever." The doctor didn't even try to argue. "Let me get the nurse and we'll get started."

Arthur didn't look away once, despite fighting to keep from being sick. Martin was covered in bruises, though most were faded to yellow and green. There were cuts held together with basic band aids insufficient to the job. For others, the doctor had to pull out makeshift stitches and put in fresh ones. And he was so damn thin.

After that, it was the waiting, no different from any other emergency room visit. Every so often a nurse would come in to check his vitals or the IV bag dripping saline, antibiotics, pain killers, and about a dozen other things into his body. As they waited, Arthur began to talk. He talked about the kids, about papers they had written comparing Jules Verne's *From the Earth to the Moon* and the actual moon mission. He talked about fluffy dinosaurs, and bits of gossip and work. His sister's dessert bistro was doing well and The Academy cinema was going to start a whole season of spaghetti westerns. There were times Martin's eyes would close and he was sure he was asleep but Arthur kept talking, making sure that even in sleep Martin would know he was there.

In between car accidents and old people having strokes it was almost six by the time they got Martin into the MRI. Arthur called in sick, even able to hold out his phone and prove he was at a hospital. He didn't mention he was at Martin's bedside. If the Agency knew, then they knew. If they didn't, then fuck them.

Doctor Keith stood at the foot of the bed flipping through reports. "Arm broken, three cracked ribs, torn knee ligaments, bruised internal organs, concussion, three different infections, I'm worried about you coming down with pneumonia, and massively underweight. But you probably knew a lot of that. I'll get someone down here to get your arm in a temporary cast, we'll do a long term one once the swelling goes down. Also, wrap up your knee. That's going to be in a brace for a while and later you will probably need surgery to repair those ligaments, and then we are getting you a room and you are staying for *at least* one more day. You do not get to argue. I'm off shift an hour ago, and you will be here when I get back on this evening, understand?" Martin and Arthur both nodded. "I don't suppose I could get a cop in here and get you to name names and press charges."

Martin gave the doctor a very confused look. "That would not be of any use."

"Worth asking. I'll see you this evening."

"You should get some sleep," Arthur said once the doctor had left. "It'll probably be an hour before anyone comes and looks at your arm."

"You should sleep as well."

"I'll try to doze in this chair if you attempt to sleep in that bed. Deal?"

Martin smiled a little. "Deal."

———

IT WAS two hours before anyone came to deal with his arm, another hour for the knee and an hour after that before an orderly wheeled Martin upstairs, Arthur following. By that time, he was hungry and trying to find someone who would sign off on a meal for the beaten, emaciated guy. He was very close to waving around his ID badge with the scary Agency logo on it.

Martin reached out and touched his arm. "Go downstairs and get yourself something to eat."

"No."

"You're hungry."

"So are you."

"I'm used to it."

Arthur sat on the edge of Martin's bed. "If I leave, how do I know you won't vanish again? How do I know you won't get a phone call, vanish for four months, and the next time I get a call from the morgue?"

"I'm not going anywhere. Not again. There were..." Martin cut himself off then took a deep breath. "I will never again be required or even asked by the Agency to set foot outside the office."

"Did they promise that?"

"Yes. And I will make them keep it."

"How?"

Martin said nothing, just smiled.

Arthur wanted to cry again. "Promise me you'll be here when I get back."

"I promise."

———

ARTHUR SPENT the afternoon mostly watching Martin doze in-between checks by the nurses and various specialists. A temporary cast was replaced with a long-term one. Neuro specialists gave him cognitive tests and tracked his eye movements. Physiotherapists and nutritionists stopped by to check and make arrangements for follow ups. Arthur was sure someone must have rattled a cage somewhere for Martin to be getting this much attention in a busy hospital. During one trip downstairs, he picked up a cheap paper-back political thriller from the gift shop, the type neither of them would ever read. He read outrageous passages aloud, doing over the top voices, until Martin finally laughed, a rare and proper one. He winced putting his hand over his cracked ribs but continued to smile.

"Have you been doing voices for the children?"

"Sometimes. They're a tough audience."

"Yes." Martin's smile softened but remained. "I missed them."

"They miss you." More than Arthur would ever be able to explain. Every week there had been questions about when Merlin was coming back and the children had quickly seen through his smiles and assurances. "You might freak them out a little if you show up all bruised.

"I shall tell them I was slaying dragons."

Arthur chuckled. He was exhausted. "Is that what you were doing? Slaying dragons?" He knew he shouldn't ask. You don't ask anyone what exactly it is they do when you work for the Agency.

"I was arranging a last-minute event for individuals with disparate personalities. It did not go well."

Arthur chuckled again, then laughed. He felt the laughter try to shift into sobs and hissed, sucking air hard through his teeth, trying to keep it all together. "Maybe you should stick to funeral planning. Maybe branch out into weddings."

"I'm not sure if I have the required personality."

"Get a bubbly receptionist and no one will notice."

Martin smiled broadly and winced at the pull on his bruised flesh, but didn't stop.

———

ARTHUR WAS half-dozing again in the hard guest chair of Martin's room when Dr. Keith walked in flipping through notes.

"Well look at this. You're still here and have not put up too much of a fuss according to the nurses. Good boys."

Arthur stood up, wincing against the protest of his stiffened muscles.

The doctor ignored him. "I want to keep you here one more day," he said to Martin.

"Why?"

"Because you have bruised kidneys and we're pumping you full of antibiotics. I want to make sure your kidneys don't shut down. I'll make a note that as long as you can still pee by tomorrow evening and all the other specialists are okay with it, you can go." Then he turned to Arthur. "You need to go home, take a shower, and get yourself some rest."

"I'm fine."

"We're going to let him out, that doesn't mean he can be on his own. Since you've been glued to his side all day, I'm going to assume you're taking him home. That means you need rest now. Go voluntarily or I'll have the nurses chuck you out."

Arthur was going to start objecting when he felt Martin's fingers on his wrist. "You should get some proper rest. I will be here when you return. Promise."

CHAPTER SIXTEEN

IT WASN'T until he got into his car that Arthur became aware of just how much he smelled and only when he saw his own bed did the exhaustion hit. He flopped onto his bed, but didn't sleep. His mind was rushing ahead, trying to make lists of all the things he had to do. The nutritionist had left a diet plan, the physiotherapists an exercise plan. They were given a long list of things Martin couldn't do for a couple of weeks with his concussion, which included reading or looking at anything on a screen. He wasn't going to like that. He grabbed his phone and sent off a quick email that he was taking another day off. He had no doubt the Agency knew exactly where he was and if the higher ups wanted to call him on it, well, he had a few things to say to them.

———

"I NEED to go into the office tomorrow." Was the first thing Martin said when Arthur stepped back into his room. It was late morning and he'd spent the day shopping for all the things Martin might need during his recovery.

"Like fuck you do. The only place you need to be is at home in bed."

"There are reports that need to be made and people—"

"You can do it from a laptop. I'll—"

"Arthur." Martin snapped. It was the first time he'd ever heard a harsh tone from him. It was a jolt and he closed his mouth with a snap of his teeth. Martin closed his eyes and let out a long sigh. "I am aware that I will not be able to fully care for myself for the next few days. I am also no longer in possession of a vehicle. I will be needing assistance." Arthur could hear the pain and frustration in his voice in admitting that he might not be entirely self-sufficient.

"Don't worry about it. I'll make sure you're okay."

"Thank you."

———

THE DOCTOR who eventually signed them out didn't look like he particularly wanted to. He gave them a long lecture about warning signs for organ failures and brain bleeding followed by an intense interrogation as to where exactly Martin would be recuperating and what was on hand. It was decided that at least for that night he would be staying with Arthur.

Physically getting out was a trick. He couldn't handle crutches with a broken arm, but even braced he couldn't put pressure on his knee without some help and he refused to use a wheelchair. A limp hop with a four-footed cane was the compromise with Arthur by his side.

He was covered in a light sheen of sweat by the time they got through the door of Arthur's, thankfully first floor, apartment. He helped Martin lower himself onto the couch. Then suddenly it was awkward. Those words Martin had spoken before he left. What he said Arthur could have. Those rambling voice mail messages. All of it hung between them.

"I'll get some dinner started."

That's right, default to food.

"I think I need a shower first."

Arthur had to agree. The sponge bath the nurses had given didn't come close to scrubbing off the layers of grime on him. "Sure. I'll show you where it is."

"I'm going to need help." Martin's voice was low and his eyes were focused on his hands.

"Of course," Arthur helped him to his feet and for the first time since he'd stumbled drunk out of Hanh's restaurant he was aware of Martin's body. His body that he kept carefully covered and would never be able to give.

He helped Martin get as far as the bathroom and sat him on the closed toilet before rushing back to the kitchen and grabbing a couple of things.

"Plastic bag and large rubber band." He held them up to Martin. "To keep the cast dry."

"Thank you."

"Lets... umm... let's get you undressed." It had been a nurse who helped Martin get into the oversized t-shirt and sweatpants since there was no way he could get the clothes he'd been brought in with over the cast and knee brace.

Get it together. He's seen you slobbering drunk. This is clinical and he needs you.

Martin raised his arms and Arthur slid off the t-shirt as carefully as he could. It was the first truly good look he'd gotten. His torso was covered in greens and yellows with a few patches still dark red. Waterproof bandages encased the stitches and there were far too many of those. There were thick scabs on his elbows and he could count every damn rib. And dirt. He was simply dirty.

He helped Martin to his feet, carefully helping him out of his pants and knee brace. His legs were no better than the rest of him. Scarred, scabbed, bruised and thin. He wished he had a chair he could put in the shower. The air wasn't cold but Martin began to shiver. He was thin before, but there wasn't a drop of fat on him now.

"Okay, let's get you in."

There was probably some great debate to be had or at least some poetry. Could you look at someone without seeing them? Touch someone without touching them? Martin didn't try to hide his body but Arthur still did his best to disconnect, somehow give him privacy in his nakedness. It wasn't easy though. Every bruise filled him with rage and the cuts raised bile in his throat. The water ran to the bottom of the tub a red brown with dirt and dried blood. A half bottle of shampoo and a bottle of body wash later,

Martin was as clean as he was likely to get and his body was shaking with the strain.

Arthur turned off the water and grabbed his largest towel. "I'm going to carry you out of here because right now I don't think you have the energy to walk."

Martin looked up at him but didn't instantly object. Arthur took that as a cue to wrap him up, carry him out, and lay him into bed. "I'm going to make dinner." He took a spare pillow to brace it under Martin's broken arm. "Try to grab a nap."

His head was already nodding and his eyes fluttering shut. "Okay."

———

IN THE kitchen, Arthur shredded cilantro by hand, ripping at the leaves and stems with all his strength. He'd held himself together as he'd scrubbed the dirt from Martin's body, watching the shriveled muscles jump and twitch when he wasn't gentle enough on bruised flesh. Now he let anger just flood him. He didn't think he could make congee aggressively, but by the time the handful of rice had cooked down into a silky porridge, he'd burned through a lot of his rage until it was just simmering worry and confusion.

A part of him had believed that when Martin returned he'd be able to simply say I understand and I accept and I love you, too. He'd said something similar in his messages, but in his fantasies Martin had reappeared by knocking on his door one night or simply turning up at work. Beaten and starved half to death in a hospital bed had not been the plan. He balanced the bowl as well as pain killers and antibiotics on the tray he usually used when he was working on his laptop in bed. Martin was fast asleep. It was tempting to leave him that way, but he needed to eat.

"Martin." He kept his voice low. "Martin. You need to eat." He put the tray aside and touched his shoulder.

Martin's whole body jolted upright, his broken arm swinging wildly. Arthur jumped back. "It's okay. It's okay. You're safe. It's Arthur and you're in my apartment and you're safe."

Martin flopped back down with a pained grunt. His lips moved slightly in what Arthur was pretty sure was a swear word.

"I'm not seven. You can say fuck in front of me."

Martin smiled then winced again.

"Okay. Let's sit you up and get you fed."

He tried to think of small talk as Martin ate and took his pills but he seemed to have used all of that in the hospital. Now the air was heavy between them, full of secrets Martin couldn't or wouldn't tell and feelings Arthur couldn't find the space to share. Martin's head nodded over the bowl. "Those painkillers are kicking in. Let's get you ready for bed before those just knock you out cold."

"Good idea."

Getting ready for bed was nearly as much of an ordeal as the shower; simple things like using the toilet and pulling on shorts and a t-shirt suddenly seeming like nearly insurmountable obstacles. Finally, he got pillows tucked in under Martin's arm and knee. "Comfortable?"

"Not really."

"I think that's as good as we're going to get for a while."

"I know."

"Okay. I'm going to be on the couch, but I'll leave the door open and-"

Martin's good hand shot out and grabbed his wrist. "Stay." Arthur just blinked at him unsure how to respond. "I know what I said but can you just, can we just—" His breath was becoming fast and agitated.

"Of course, Yes." Arthur answered. He would love nothing more than to lay next to Martin, feel him close, know he was there. "Let me just clean up the dishes." Martin nodded and let go of his wrist.

Arthur's hands shook as he loaded the dishwasher. He'd thought a lot about a relationship with Martin while he was gone. At least in that first month before the panic really set in. He'd flitted around the idea of sharing a bed. He was fairly certain Martin was asexual, but there was so much more physical contact possible before sex even came into the equation. Could they hug?

Would he want to cuddle? Would he want to share a bed or sleep separately? He'd decided that he would be glad with Martin's heart and head, both amazing. Those things would outlast any physical relationship anyhow. But this would still be close. Just a couple layers of thin fabric between them was closer than anyone had gotten to Arthur in years.

He took his time brushing his teeth and getting ready for bed, calming himself as much as he could.

Martin seemed to be asleep as he slipped in. His bed wasn't large and with Martin tucked in closer to the middle, there was no way he couldn't touch. Even if he crunched himself up, as soon as he fell asleep everything would relax. His arm brushed against Martin's.

Martin opened his eyes and turned his head. "It's okay. This is okay."

Arthur nodded and in exhaustion instantly fell asleep.

CHAPTER SEVENTEEN

HE'D SET his alarm for the standard work time since, in theory, they were going to work. It still hurt when it went off. Arthur fumbled for his phone, cursing the swipe screen that never seemed to want to register first thing in the morning. Once the beeping stopped, he rolled over to look at Martin, who was already staring at him.

"How much do you hurt?" he asked first.

"Not as much as yesterday." His voice was rough.

"That's not saying much."

"No."

"Still need to go to the office?"

"Yes."

Arthur sighed, expecting the answer but hoping for different.

"Okay. I grabbed one of your suits from your apartment, but there's no way you're getting into it unless you want to cut off the sleeves and the legs. Could be an interesting fashion statement..."

Martin made a face at him.

"I did a bit of shopping yesterday. I got you some loose sweats and t-shirts, some shorts if you really want to freak people out. I think you should freak people out."

This time Martin smiled a little.

———

THE SHORTS and t-shirt were decided on, accessorized with a blue sling, less for freak-out value and more for ease of dressing and undressing. It was still a shocking look, bruises, bandages, a bloodshot eye and skinny wrists. Security did a triple take as Martin scanned his ID card with Arthur right behind. The whispers ran ahead of them with people glancing out of their cubicles to see the spectacle. The long missing alien and his heartbroken boyfriend. There were two men in dark suits waiting in Martin's cubicle. They dismissed Arthur with a wave, but he didn't move. Instead he found his hand balling into a fist wanting to punch whoever was responsible for sending someone obviously not a field agent into a four-month hell.

He gently touched Arthur's shoulder. "I just need to take a few meetings. I'll meet you for lunch."

Arthur nodded. "Okay." It wasn't okay. Not even remotely okay. But this was the Agency and things were what they were. He took a bottle of antibiotics from his pocket and pressed it into Martin's hand, their fingers brushing. "Two at ten with lots of water."

"Thank you."

At his desk, he found dozens of emails waiting, the typical mess when you take a couple of sick days. He heard Martin and the dark suited men walk slowly down the hall. Arthur gritted his teeth and got to work.

———

MARTIN WAS waiting for him in the lunch room. It was almost as if he'd never been gone. Almost. People glanced at him then quickly looked away. Martin's eyes were closed and he was rubbing his head. It was more reaction and emotion than he'd expressed in this room, ever.

"Are you okay?" Arthur asked as he sat down. "I should have given you the painkillers before you left."

Martin shook his head. "Just a headache. A lot of reading in a short space of time."

"You're not supposed to read with a concussion."

"I am aware."

Arthur unpacked their lunch. Peanut butter and jam sandwich for Martin with a fruit smoothie. Fat, protein, vitamins. He ate slowly, with small twitches of pain around his eyes when he moved too fast. Arthur wanted to pick him up and take him home. A half day work was surely enough for them both.

"I have more meetings," he volunteered "But then I have two weeks off for my head to heal."

"Good."

"They're going to be very boring weeks."

"I'll read to you. I'll even do the voices."

Martin chuckled and every head in the room turn their way.

———

ARTHUR PUSHED open the door to Martin's apartment. "I dusted, brought in your mail, cleaned out the fridge so there's nothing weird growing in it."

"Thank you."

"I'll go stick this in the fridge." He lifted the bags of groceries they'd picked up on the way back. He would have preferred to go back to his place, but Martin wanted to get back to his own apartment. He understood. When he stepped out of the kitchen, he expected to find Martin sitting at the single seat table but it was empty.

"Martin?" He peeked into the living room. Martin was seated on the floor against the wall across from the painting. Arthur said nothing more, just took a seat on the floor beside him. The picture was beautiful in its way, once he looked close. The Lautrec cancan girls had been mass produced for so long, it was easy to overlook them, but there was a flow to the dress that contrasted with the sharp lines of the dancer's legs.

"You said your great grandmother?" He had a hard time picturing Martin with any direct family, but somehow the idea of a cancan dancer in a haze of smoke and perfume fit.

Martin shook his head. "The last individual directly responsible for my care was a woman of means and an eye for beauty. She loved art. This was her favorite as she believed it to be one of her great grandmothers."

"She gave it to you?"

"When she passed, her estranged husband returned to the house to collect the art. And throw me out. He knew nothing about it, only that it was valuable. This was laying on the floor, sticking out from between a Monet sketch and an early Picasso. I tucked it under my arm and walked out the front door."

"Not afraid he's ever going to come looking for it."

"He was recently executed for the particularly brutal and sadistic murder of his estranged wife and her lover."

Arthur didn't respond. He had a feeling that if he looked up executions from the last year he would find one that would line up with the day Martin spent staring at a bottle of gin, not drinking it. It would also be the key to everything else. With his access, he could look up the victim. Martin would almost certainly be mentioned somewhere in the investigation and from there, back tracking through school records, family services maybe, whatever might have his name on it. Martin had to know he just told Arthur how to find everything.

"Martin." Martin turned and looked at him. He put a hand over his own heart. "This is yours." He placed his fingers to his forehead. "So is this. You can have the rest if you're ever interested, but if not, that's okay too." He reached out and gently touched Martin's chest. "This is more important."

Martin placed his hand over Arthur's, pressing it to his chest. He could feel the pounding of his heart. "Thank you." His voice was a rough whisper.

Arthur turned his hand around and laced their fingers together. He could feel his own heart rushing in his chest as Martin's fingers entwined with his. Better than a fumbled kiss or faked affection. It was strong and true. And it was theirs.

AN AGENCY
SHORT STORY

Merlin
IN THE LIBRARY

Ada Maria Soto

MERLIN IN THE LIBRARY

An Agency Short Story

Martin clenched his hands into fists, trying to drive away the last paralysis of sleep. His heart raced at full speed as dreams, interwoven with too recent memories, slid from his waking mind. He unclenched his hands and instead pressed his thumbs and ringfingers together. It was supposed to be grounding.

'Breath in, hold, breathe out.' He repeated trying to calm his breath. He didn't want to wake Arthur. His internal clock wasn't what it had been, but he knew it was early from the orange street light still peaking from between the curtains.

He tried closing his eyes and settling into the softness of Arthur's bed and the simple comfortable warmth of Arthur's body next to his, but it didn't work. There were too many little flashes of memories still sparking across his mind.

The previous day had been bad on the pain scale, leaving him with little appetite. Now, under the persistent ache, he found himself to be hungry. He would have to get up. Doctor's orders, if he was hungry he needed to eat. He also had to make notes of dreams, flashbacks, or intrusive thoughts. Orders from more doctors. He'd nearly lost count of how many doctors and specialists had say over some aspect of his life. At least the Agency was paying for them. Better to eat first. If he did that he could possibly take one of his milder pain pills and get back to sleep.

He pushed back the blankets as carefully as he could and tried to slowly roll from the bed, gritting his teeth as he did. He'd found that as one injury healed he would discover another that had been masked. Placing his feet on the floor sent a dull pain from his toes to his hips. Still he kept quiet. He didn't want to wake Arthur. He'd caused the man enough sleepless nights already. He grabbed the cane that was leaning against his bedside table

It was a longer walk from Arthur's bedroom to his kitchen than in Martin's own apartment, but Arthur's fridge was far better stocked.

The throbbing in his hip had noticeably increased by the time he'd gotten to the kitchen, but as he spotted the fridge the grumble in his stomach turned from light hunger to its own kind of pain. He swallowed hard and breathed. More intrusive thoughts, memories of clawing hunger strong enough to break even his self-control.

He opened the fridge and blinked into the harsh light. Arthur had stocked it with foods he could simply eat, standing right there. He could be sated in seconds and go back to bed. Instead his eyes lingered on the jar of mustard and a block of gruyere cheese. His mind felt as unsettled as his stomach.

He pulled ingredients from the fridge. This he knew, better than any other recipe, the first thing Arthur had taught him to cook. The first thing he had ever learned to cook that did not involve reading instructions from the side of a box or can. "Fancy French grilled cheese," Arthur had told him at the time.

It was also the memory he'd used when he'd needed to escape deep into his own mind. He would carefully reconstruct it. The sharp smell of the cheese and sourdough bread. The pressure of the knife against the still cool butter and the way it stuck to the edge of the blade before going in the pan. The feel of the ridges of the wrapped wire whisk pressing into the side of his finger. The sound of the whisk through the milk and the way it changed as the sauce thickened. And Arthur, there beside him, patient and thoughtful, laughing bright when his own sauce burnt through lack of attention.

He pressed the power button on the oven. Like everything at this hour, it seemed far too loud. The pain in his hip persisted. He wanted to sit but he also wanted to cook. The urge to create for himself was almost as strong as the hunger. He pulled a copper pot from a hook over the bench and tried to place it silently on the stove, but his arm was still weak and the pot was heavier than he remembered. It clanged against the metal and he winced at the noise.

"Need a hand?"

Martin turned towards the words. Arthur was blinking in the light, hair mussed, a strange pattern from the wrinkled pillow case pressed into his cheek.

"I'm sorry I woke you up."

Arthur smiled at him. "It's okay. Can I help?"

Martin wanted to reassure Arthur that he was fine and send him back to bed, except his therapist reminded him every session that there was nothing wrong in asking for help and he should do so whenever he felt the need. This advice was anathema to the way he had lived his life. Before. But that was then. He was, if nothing else, not stupid. He knew he was on a long road and stubbornness was only going to make it longer.

"If you could assemble the sandwich."

"No problem. Your hip okay?"

"Yes," Martin lied. He was already giving half the job to Arthur. He wanted to make the cream sauce himself. He wanted to feel the warm heat of the pan and witness the subtle chemistry of butter, flour, and milk. They were real and tangible things that would serve to remind him of where he was and what he was still capable of doing.

Arthur sat at the table and began assembling sandwiches. Ham and cheese with a subtle scrape of mustard. Martin dropped butter into the bottom of the pan and watched it begin to slowly melt. The first time they had cooked this together, Arthur had given him precise measurements of weights and volumes. The second time Arthur had insisted he learn how to gauge the proportions by eye. He likened it to a musician being able to play a piece by ear.

The butter melted and Martin slowly whisked in the flour, a spoonful at a time. The rising heat was soothing. There was a hiss and a quick puff of steam as he poured in the milk. He whisked quickly like Arthur had taught him. His hands ached slightly but not enough to risk burning the sauce.

"We could put a fried egg on these. Make them into croque madames. Or is that a little rich at this hour?"

Martin watched the butter and milk begin to thicken into a thick creamy sauce. As hungry as he was, he still couldn't handle too much food or anything too heavy. There was a chance he'd end up regretting the ham and cheese as it was. "I think the egg might be too much for now."

Arthur just hummed in agreement and said nothing more. Arthur seldom, if ever, pushed for more or pressed himself in where he was unwanted. Yet somehow, he had slid himself so fully and naturally into Martin's life that when they were separated, his absence was felt as keenly as any physical pain.

He turned off the stove and let the sauce finish on the residual heat.

Arthur brought over two sandwiches on a baking tray and Martin carefully poured the sauce over them before they were slipped into the hot oven.

"Why don't you sit down. I'll wash the pot."

Martin only nodded, knowing he was on the verge of severely exacerbating his knee. Arthur could probably tell. He would have to put the brace on before going to the library.

It didn't take long for the sandwiches to brown and for Arthur to plate them. It was something Martin had noticed early, when he was still trying to figure out the man who sat across from him at lunch, the way Arthur took time to present everything he made, even if it was just for himself. It wasn't elaborate and covered in garnish, but there was always a sense of care.

Martin's stomach growled audibly as he cut into the croque monsieur and a shock of emotion rocked his body at the taste. He closed his eyes and chewed slowly, trying to fight back tears, remembering the peaceful fun he felt the first time he'd had this and not the months of fear that he would never again sit beside Arthur and share a meal.

He knew he shouldn't be trying to repress emotions at this point in the process, but he was already tired and he was afraid a long and wracking cry would simply take too much out of him and he actually had plans for the morning. He took long breaths in between bites.

"You doing okay?"

Martin nodded. "I'm... here." It was something he reminded himself of several times a day.

"Yes, you are." Arthur's hand momentarily covered his. "Have you decided what you're telling the kids yet?"

As desperate as he had been to slip back into his routine of Saturday story time at the library, he had not wanted to subject the children to the full extent of his injuries. The concussions had also left him prone to nodding off and unable to read for more than a few minutes without developing a severe headache. His face, at least, was down to some yellowed bruises. "I think I'll stick with telling them I was slaying dragons."

"Slaying dragons. They'll like that."

Arthur's voice was soft. Martin wanted to tell him the truth, to cry and scream and try to explain, but it was classified and sealed well beyond Arthur's rank. The size of the "bonus" in his bank account and the lack of medical bills showed just how much the Agency wanted to not be reminded of how badly they had screwed up to leave Martin in the middle of a high-level trade with no back-up and inadequate information.

"You may have to do the reading for a few more weeks," Martin admitted.

"I can manage. Just as long as you're there."

———

The heavy double doors of the library hissed slightly, like an airlock. Inside it was cool and dry and still smelled of aging books and fresh newspapers. Martin breathed deeply. It was another sense memory he had clung onto and buried himself in when he needed to escape the realities of his situation. He'd been afraid that it would have changed somehow in his absence, either some small detail that was important to him would have been changed or the city would have figured out how to strip the last of the funding and he would return to nothing but rubble. In the moments when he had believed he would return.

But there was no rubble. Everything was the same, right down to the collection of old men flipping through newspapers, peering at them through drug store reading glasses.

"Ready?" Arthur asked him softly.

Martin nodded in reply.

Still leaning heavily on his cane and Arthur holding his books, he slowly made his way to the circulation counter.

Amy, the rare books librarian, looked up as they approached. The squeak she let out echoed through the stacks. Martin smiled and she grinned. He'd been finding it easier to smile, just in general. He wondered if that was the result of the Agency mandated therapy or simply hitting a point of no longer caring about what the general population might think of him.

Amy rushed from behind her desk. She started to raise her arms slightly as if to hug him but her eyes fell on the cane, brace, and bruises. Instead she took the books from Arthur. "The children are going to be so happy to see you."

"Are they here?"

"I think I've seen most of them go by." The children's section had its own entrance, but Martin had always encouraged them to go up the marble stairs and push open the grand doors. He never wanted them in the habit of sneaking in a side door when they could go through the front.

"I should get started, then."

Martin was sure the children's section was not that far from the circulation desk, but by the time he reached the bright annex a fine sweat had broken out across his body and he could feel an ache in nearly every joint and muscle.

"Merlin!" It was Esmerelda who spotted him. There was a rush, like puppies, banging into and tripping over each other. The children slowed as they approached, really looking at him, but Martin spread his arms. Esmerelda hugged him first. The bruises over his still cracked ribs throbbed and his knees burned as he crouched down. The next hug he got hurt even worse. It felt like his ribs might get pushed right into his lungs. He didn't care. He took each hug and squeezed back as hard as his broken and aching body would let him.

"Where have you been?" Miguel finally asked, once every child had been held tight.

"Slaying dragons," Martin answered and heard the crack in his own voice. "If you think this is bad, you should see the dragon."

The children smiled but he could see wariness in their eyes as they looked him over. He knew many had their own familiarity with violence and used the library as a refuge from that reality.

"Are you going to be slaying any more dragons?" Miguel asked.

"No." As a whole, the children relaxed. "Quite done with dragons." He started to move towards the adult sized chair before his legs could go out from under him. "However, Arthur will still be doing the reading for a few more weeks, and I have not yet had the chance to go through all your papers."

"Do you have a concussion?" one of the youngest children asked.

Martin grunted softly as he sat but hopefully kept the full extent of discomfort off his face. "Yes." Several of the children nodded in understanding. "However, that is not a valid reason to have any lapses in your own studies. I have hopes, and plans, for all of you and I intend to be here to see them through, but you have to do your part as well. So, homework."

He held out his hand and papers were handed forward.

"We read *A Sound of Thunder,* and discussed how even small actions by people, intentional or unintentional can have great effect on the world."

"I look forward to reading them." And he did. Since that first time he stumbled into a library at age ten, cold, wet, and lost in New York, reading had been the cornerstone of his life. The fractured bones were not half as frustrating as the fracturing of his daily reading.

Arthur picked up a ragged paperback from the shelf and opened it to a bookmarked page. "Today's story is called *The Great Wide World Over There* and is actually about reading or not, which was something of great importance to Ray Bradbury."

The children settled themselves and Arthur began to read.

Martin watched the children as they focused on Arthur's words. They were all taller. He'd noticed that. Some days it felt as if he had been gone for years and at other times, just moments. During the long stretches, when he'd been left alone, he would bring each child to mind. He would force himself to remember their face and voice and their handwriting, then he would plan. He'd been meticulous in his research. He'd picked schools for them, followed by universities. And after that internships and fellowships, eventually bringing rational thought into the highest levels of the public and private sectors. He always knew it was silly. You can't plan out the life of a child. They must make their own decisions and become their own people eventually, but that didn't mean he couldn't nudge them this way or that. They called him Merlin after all and what did Merlin do but nudge minds this way or that?

He felt himself fade out, losing himself in the melody of Arthur's voice and missing parts of the story. He would ask Arthur to reread it tonight if possible. The specialists told him it could take years for his brain to fully heal from the repeated knocks he'd received. Seven serious ones that he could remember. It left him little doubt that he would have to leave the Agency at some point, but not until he had taken full advantage of the health insurance. They owed him that much.

It also gave him time to consider the next steps in his life as opposed to simply clinging to the first situation that offered, at least the illusion of, stability. Arthur said he should teach, and the thought did hold some appeal. It wouldn't be the same as these Saturdays though. Here he had freedom to teach what and as he wished and the children, in turn, came to him of their own free will. No requirements or expectations on either side.

Arthur closed the book. "Okay, what are your initial thoughts?"

The children were quiet for a minute mulling around their own thoughts.

"The lady put all that effort into making it look like she could read and write, why didn't she use that time *actually* learning to read and write?" Daniel, who usually sat at the front of the group, asked.

"That is a very good question," Arthur replied. "Does anyone have an idea?"

"Maybe she tried before and couldn't?"

"Possibly."

Martin smiled as the discussion continued, Arthur guiding but not lecturing, and making sure the quieter children had space to talk. He was proud. It had been a fevered moment of need, and perhaps a childish prank, that had him sending Arthur to the library the first time, but he had stepped in and done well.

Arthur began to wrap up the conversation. "Time for the quote of the week. Maybe Merlin should get to pick it out of the box."

The decorated box of scraps of paper was held out to him. He picked one and read it. "Yes: I am a dreamer. For a dreamer is one who can only find his way by moonlight, and his punishment is that he sees the dawn before the rest of the world. Oscar Wilde, The Critic as Artist"

"Oscar Wilde, a man who was beloved for his writing until he fell afoul of the harsh morality laws of his time. Maybe we should try one of his plays next week. You can all play the parts and read to us instead." The children smiled and nodded. "Okay, pack up and for homework I want you to think about literacy as a status symbol."

The children got up and almost as one turned to Martin. "Are you going to be back next week?"

He saw the unease in their eyes again. "Yes. No more dragon slaying. I promise." And he would keep that promise, even if it meant walking away from the Agency sooner than intended. They had made him promises but he knew that the right changes in upper management could break those promises as easily as they were made.

The clean-up was finalized by another round of hugs which hurt as much as the first, but again he could not bring himself to care.

By the time he got to the car his heart was thumping and he felt another thin sweat across his body. He closed his eyes and let himself sink into the passenger seat of Arthur's car. Hardly a luxury model, it still felt like the seat was molding around him in comfort.

Arthur got into the driver's seat. "Home?"

Martin shook his head. "Could we have dumplings? If there is time?" He was still getting used to asking for things he wanted as opposed to providing for himself the bare minimum of what he needed.

"Sure, if you think you're up for it?"

"As long as we don't walk much, I think I can manage." Of the many habits and routines shattered by his time away, lunch after story time was the one he felt would be the easiest to get back into.

Arthur drove them the handful of blocks to the Rabbit Moon Dumpling House. It was one of the first places Arthur had taken him and where he had learned, if not fully mastered, how to use chopsticks. He wondered if he had managed to maintain the fine dexterity needed or if he would have to go back to a fork for a time.

The waitress, whom he didn't recognize, only glanced at him briefly before directing her attention to Arthur. That had been one of the harder things to get used to over the last few weeks as he started to venture out again; the lack of anonymity combined with an appearance that put people off. Not that he went out much before, but when he did no one stared. He reminded himself that he would heal, he was already healing, and the scars that were unavoidable would be mostly out of sight. He just needed to be patient.

They were lead to a table for two and handed menus while another waitress put down cups and a pot of tea.

"Craving anything in particular?" Arthur asked him.

Martin shook his head. "You can choose." Arthur knew what he liked. If he was craving anything, it was the ability to sit in a restaurant on a Saturday afternoon. It was something he had never done in his adult life prior to meeting Arthur, but he'd developed a fondness for it.

Arthur poured the tea. The steam rose up smelling floral and a little bitter. Martin wrapped his hands around his cup and held them there until the heat came close to pain. Arthur blew on his and sipped it quietly until the waitress came over to take their orders. Again, she made only the briefest of eye contact before Arthur began to order. Martin wondered what she must be thinking: car accident, fight, victim of random violence?

Arthur ordered a half-dozen items from the menu before taking another sip of tea. "I was thinking, maybe next month swinging back to the classics. Epic poetry."

"They did enjoy Beowulf."

"Yeah, but we can go broader. I'm sure plenty of those kids applying for those fancy schools know Beowulf or the Illiad. I was thinking more the Mahabharata. Well, sections of it. It has two hundred thousand verses as I recall from my world lit class. Maybe something from South East Asia. Lots of epics from that region."

Martin nodded in agreement. It was a good idea and it made him glad that Arthur took his plans for the children seriously. He'd spent large parts of his life with no one to voice his thoughts or ideas to, leaving him wondering how rational or practical they really were. But self-doubt could be a killer, literally, if it came at the wrong moment.

"We can request a suitable translation from Amy next week."

The waitress put a bowl of eggs on the table. Their shells were mottled brown. Martin picked one up. It was warm in his hands.

"They're called tea eggs. They've been boiled in tea and spices."

Martin turned the egg in his fingers and a memory tugged at the edges of his mind. Not a recent one. Old. So old. Brown eggs, still warm, almost too large for small hands. Gentle voices over the sounds of chickens. A sandy path and feet bare. Flickers of sunlight through the branches of fruit trees. The smell of warm bread.

"Martin?"

Martin looked up from the egg. He wasn't sure how long he'd been staring at his hands. "When I was small my mother and I lived with..."

'A cult. It was a cult. Just say it.'

"A spiritually-centered agricultural-based community. It was my job to collect the eggs, first thing in the morning, when the chickens were still half asleep. The eggs were always brown. I was very confused the first time I saw a white egg. I thought it must have come from some strange bird, like a swan."

Arthur reached across the table and placed his hands around Martin's and the egg. "Thank you for sharing that with me."

The waitress put a plate of dumplings between them and Arthur let go. Martin wanted to say more. He could. There was no reason for any of it to be a secret. There never was. He opened his mouth to explain but nothing came out.

'Not yet, I guess.'

Small steps. Little pieces. He honestly couldn't remember when he'd last spent any time thinking about the farm. Not since those first terrifying months in his aunt's elegant, Manhattan apartment where everything had been alien, from the noise, to the people, to the stench of the air. Her staff had tried to comfort him with broken English and foods like nothing he'd ever experienced.

"Do you know how to make...?" he wracked his tear-streaked memories. "A soup. It has chicken, and green papaya, I think? And it's spicy."

Arthur smiled at him and Martin felt like he was standing in a shaft of sun between rustling trees. "It doesn't ring a bell. But I bet we can look it up and make it together."

ABOUT THE AUTHOR

Ada Maria Soto is a Mexican/American expat living in the South Pacific. She's a veteran of the theatre and film business as well as all the lousy jobs that come with two liberal arts degrees. A psychologist once told her she has a fantasy prone personality, but since she's trying to be a writer that's not a bad thing. She is a fan of rugby, cricket, and baseball, who loves to cook, knit, and poke around her garden.

You can find her online at http://adamariasoto.com/ and on most social media platforms.

Her previous, award winning work, can be found on most online book sellers.

ALSO BY ADA MARIA SOTO

Windsor Club

Tactical Submission

Triple Windsor

The Agency

His Quiet Agent (Audio Book)

Merlin in the Library

Nested Hearts

Empty Nests

Bower Birds

Eden Springs

Through the Dark Clouds

Life Saving Dal